Friends?

It was such a pale word for the way she'd once thought of him. Soul mate was closer. Lover even more accurate. But it had started with friendship. Did she dare allow it to start like that again, when she knew the feelings that still stirred inside her at the sight of him?

"I think it would be a mistake," she said at last. "Wasn't it some ancient philosopher who once said that 'even God can't change the past'?"

"I don't want to change it. I just want to learn to live with it," Steven insisted.

"I've lived with it every day for the last eleven years. I don't need you reminding me of it. It's far too late for friendship now. Just go on with your life and let me go on with mine."

"I don't think I can do that, sweetheart. Not anymore." He took a step toward her.

"Stop it," Lara pleaded. "Stop saying that. You left, Steven. You betrayed me. You betrayed all of us. You can never change that. It's too late. I don't want you back."

As if her words had been a challenge, a slow, gentle smile, brighter now, tugged at the corners of his lips. "I'll make you want me again, Lara. You know I can do it, don't you?"

Dear Reader:

Happy New Year!

It takes two to tango, and we've declared 1989 as the "Year of the Man" at Silhouette Desire. We're honoring that perfect partner, the magnificent male, the one without whom there would *be* no romance. January marks the beginning of a twelve-month extravaganza spotlighting one book each month as a tribute to the Silhouette Desire hero—our *Man of the Month*!

Created by your favorite authors, you'll find these men are utterly irresistible. You'll be swept away by Diana Palmer's Mr. January (whom some might remember from a brief appearance in *Fit for a King*), and Joan Hohl's Mr. February is every woman's idea of the perfect Valentine....

Don't let these men get away!

Yours,

Isabel Swift
Senior Editor & Editorial Coordinator

SHERRYL WOODS
Heartland

Silhouette Desire

Published by Silhouette Books New York

America's Publisher of Contemporary Romance

SILHOUETTE BOOKS
300 East 42nd St., New York, N.Y. 10017

ISBN: 0-373-05472-6

First Silhouette Books printing January 1989

Books by Sherryl Woods

Silhouette Desire

Not at Eight, Darling #309
Yesterday's Love #329
Come Fly with Me #345
A Gift of Love #375
Can't Say No #431
Heartland #472

Silhouette Special Edition

Safe Harbor #425
Never Let Go #446
Edge of Forever #484

SHERRYL WOODS

lives by the ocean, which, she says, provides daily inspiration for the romance in her soul. She further explains that her years as a television critic taught her about steamy plots and humor; her years as a travel editor took her to exotic locations; and her years as a crummy weekend tennis player taught her to stick with what she enjoyed most—writing. "What better way is there," Sherryl asks, "to combine all that experience than by creating romantic stories?"

Prologue

November, 1986

From the top of the knoll, Lara's gaze swept over the barren winter landscape. Gnarled oaks stood stark but proud against the leaden sky. Flat, snow-covered fields stretched as far as the eye could see. For some it would be a scene of incomparable desolation. To her the view held beauty and simplicity and grace. Yet, undeniably, there was also heartache.

Struck anew by the sorrow that had come hand in hand with the fleeting moments of joy, she wrapped her arms tightly around her waist. The shiver that ran through her came as much from the memories as from the icy wind. Lost in those memories, she surveyed the harsh land that had been her home for nearly twenty-six years, and she wept.

This land had killed her father, its demanding temperament too great a match for his ailing heart. It bore its share of blame for her mother's death as well, robbing her of the strength that might have made her fight against pneumonia a fair one.

As a teenager Lara had hated the farm, hated the endless chores and cruel winds, hated the loneliness and, most of all, the bitter victories it had claimed against her family. Only an ironic twist of fate had brought her back, a promise made in desperation, a last bargain made with a god who hadn't heard her pleas for her mother's life after all.

"Please, Lara, keep the family together," her mother had begged. "Keep the farm. It's your legacy. It's what your father would have wanted."

"You'll keep us together, Mama. You'll do it," she had said.

Feverish eyes burned into her soul. "Promise, Lara."

Broken at last by her mother's quiet pleading, she had made the promise. Then she had watched in dismay and horror as her mother slipped quietly away.

For four years now she had done her best to keep her pledge. She had left college to do it. She had seen her brothers grow from skinny, awkward boys into strong young men ready to begin lives of their own. With them she had worked the fields from dawn to dusk in spring and summer, hired help when she could afford it and hauled her crops to market in Toledo. Her hands, which she'd once hoped would have the healing touch of a doctor, were raw and rough now, and her brothers—Tommy and Greg—would have the chances she had lost.

"I did it, Mama," she said, the words torn away by the wind. "We made it."

There was pride as well as bitterness in the claim. The accomplishment, though not of her own choosing, was a worthy one. Against the odds, she had eked out a living. The bank had been lenient, granting extensions on the loans her father had taken out time and again to survive. The debts, if she'd stopped to really consider them, would have swallowed her last vestige of hope.

Through the struggle she had gained an appreciation of this farm and what it had meant to her father. She had understood at last why he had fought so hard to hold onto it, keeping the developers who would have bought him out at bay. She had come to love the farm's daily challenges, its tiring demands and satisfying routines. She had come to respect the mighty quirks of nature that could destroy on a whim all that it had taken months to attain. Despite the resentment for chances lost, with a slow inevitability the farm had done what she'd thought impossible: it had claimed her heart.

Slowly she turned and went back to the house. She warmed her hands at the fireplace before gathering her things for the trip into town that would determine whether, after all she'd endured to keep it, the farm would remain hers.

At the bank Lara took a deep breath before entering Mr. Hogan's intimidating, mahogany-paneled office. The visit had been an annual one for four years now, but it had never gotten any easier. Though the bank president had been kind, that very kindness had been like the rubbing of salt in a wound. Her pride, that staunch Danvers' pride her father had instilled in her, had taken a beating each time she had been forced to admit that she needed yet another extension on the loans. This time would be no different.

As she stepped through the doorway, though, trepidation fled, replaced at once by something else entirely. Her gaze was immediately drawn to the impressively built man seated across from the bank president. Brown hair, a week or two beyond the need for a cut, skimmed the collar of a beige shirt. Thick, curling hair that was all too familiar. Her heart, already fluttering nervously, thundered wildly in recognition. As he stood slowly at her entrance and turned toward her, she had to fight to control the wrenching panic that invaded her.

Steven Drake.

It had been nearly eight years since she'd seen him last, and to her utter chagrin, he still possessed the power to stir her senses. Though he was wearing an expensive suit, which had been tailored to fit his powerful shoulders perfectly, he still had the rugged appearance of a man more at ease in denim and flannel. The hand that clasped hers was as callused and hard as her own, but gentler somehow than she'd remembered, as though he'd learned restraint to match his strength.

"Lara," he said. There was a lifetime of raw emotion in his voice—pain, entreaty, desire—all in that single, softly spoken word. Eyes as blue as a brilliant winter sky caressed her with a summer's warmth, yet Lara shivered as she had on the knoll.

Years ago Steven Drake had taken the innocent world of an eighteen-year-old girl and turned it upside down. He had taught her about the incomparable beauty of love, then ruined it with a lesson in betrayal. Was it possible he was back to do it again? Something told her that the tentative friendliness of his smile and the warmth in his eyes hid a chilling purpose. It took less than a minute for the bank president to confirm that this meeting had taken place by design, not chance.

"Sit down, Lara. I hope you don't mind if Mr. Drake joins us."

She could tell from his brisk tone that it wasn't a question. He'd invited Steven, and she was expected to acquiesce to his presence. He folded his hands on top of the desk and stared at them for what seemed an eternity. Then he cleared his throat. She had known Richard Hogan for years, since she'd begun coming to the bank with her father when she was no more than five or six. He was a dignified, humorless man, but he'd always been kind. Even at the age of five, though, she had sensed his power. He wielded it with restraint but wore it in a way that emphasized its presence nonetheless. In all these years this was the first hint of nervousness she'd ever witnessed in him. Ironically it filled her with dread.

"Lara, my dear," he began at last. "The payment on your loan is due today. Can you make it?"

Steven watched her closely, his observance rattling her far more than she cared to admit. She swallowed hard and lifted her chin defiantly. Ignoring him, she told Mr. Hogan, "I have most of it." She handed him a sizable check, more than she'd ever been able to pay before.

He glanced at it. "What about the rest?"

She felt her body go rigid with tension. She'd been so sure he would be impressed by the amount. Furious at the need for humility and dismayed that Steven was there as a witness, she found herself pleading for continued patience.

"Please, I'm sure if you can give me a few more weeks I'll have it. I've taken a job for the winter, and my brothers are working while they're at college. Tommy will graduate at the end of the semester and get a full-time job, in addition to helping out at the farm. Greg's already selling some of his paintings and sending the extra money home."

"Art is hardly a reliable income," he pointed out. "And Tommy has his own family to consider now. Besides, I thought he was studying business, not agriculture."

"He is, but he and Megan have agreed to stay on at the farm until it's on its feet. There's plenty of room for them and the baby. It'll help them out, too. We can do it, Mr. Hogan. This will be the last year I'll have to ask for an extension. With a good crop next year, the farm will finally be in the black."

The two men exchanged a look.

"Perhaps I have a solution," Steven offered.

Lara felt her heart begin to pound again, and her hands instinctively clenched into fists. Facing Mr. Hogan and never once allowing her eyes to stray to the man seated next to her, she asked the question that had been uppermost in her mind since she'd entered the room: "Why is he here?"

Unaware of the undercurrents or, more likely, simply misjudging their cause, Mr. Hogan said, "Mr. Drake would like to help you out, Lara. We've already talked about this quite a bit. Give him a chance to explain."

"This is between you and me, Mr. Hogan. It's bank business. We don't need an outsider to settle it."

"Yes, my dear. I think we do."

Lara couldn't bear the look of pity in Mr. Hogan's eyes, but the alternative would be to face Steven, and she wasn't sure she could stand that, either.

"I want to buy some of your land," Steven said.

The offer hung in the air, a temptation and a curse.

"No." The retort was instinctively sharp, unyielding.

"Why, Lara? Is it that stubborn pride of yours?"

She faced him at last, eyes blazing. "How dare you ask me that when you did your best to strip me of my pride?" she said flaring. "This was my father's land and his father's before him. He turned you down eight years ago. I'm not about to go against his wishes. That's not just pride, that's conviction and loyalty, things you know nothing about."

He met her furious gaze, and she saw something in his eyes that confused her. A softening. Perhaps even regret. He didn't deny her charges but said simply, "Hear me out, Lara. Please."

She couldn't listen, not when his presence set off a wild churning inside her, not when his words could be no more than lies. She had had more than enough of Steven Drake's lies.

"I said no. There's nothing you can say that would make me reconsider. Wasn't it bad enough that you used me to try to get the land away from my father? Did you have to come back to rub my face in it? Have you been waiting all this time for your chance to steal the land from us, the way you did from the others?" She glared at him. "I'd rather declare bankruptcy than sell you one square inch of Danvers land."

A tiny muscle worked in his jaw, but his voice was calm, patient, reasonable. So damned reasonable.

"Then you'd only lose the whole farm," he said. "With my way, you'll keep some of it. You could go back to school yourself, Lara. All those dreams you had, they could still come true. You wouldn't have to stay tied to the farm forever."

"The farm is my life now. Those were just the foolish dreams of a girl."

"Not so foolish," he said. The words were a whispered reminder of so much that had been lost. Steven had always understood her dreams, encouraged them. Or so she had thought. She'd had eight long years to examine his motives without the gloss of infatuation. The dreams and her faith had been turned to ashes the night he abandoned her without a word. She'd been left with nothing but silence and regret.

"Listen to him, Lara," Mr. Hogan pleaded now. "It's a sensible solution for all of you."

Unable to stop the outpouring of words, she listened, her heart heavy. Steven's solution was, indeed, sensible. His payment for the hundred acres of woods down along the stream would clear the family of debt and keep the farm afloat for several years. Best of all, he pointed out, it would not take any of the farm-land.

No, Lara thought, it would just take the most pic-turesque portion of the property, land that filled only Lara's frivolous need for someplace calm and sooth-ing, a refuge at the end of those long, backbreaking summer days. He wanted only the section where they had made love under a midnight sky, an act that ob-viously had held no meaning for him, while it had changed her life.

"What would you do with the land?" she asked, her voice laced with years of pent-up scorn. "Put in some housing project?"

"Only my own home."

"For now."

"For all time."

The deal in the end was made, because there was no choice. Mr. Hogan had made that quite clear. Too many small family farms were failing. The bank was being forced to foreclose.

"Don't lose it all, Lara," he advised. "Not when you have this chance to save it."

And Steven was true to his word. Only his own home—a house of wood and stone on a slope of vel-vet green lawn surrounded by acres of towering trees—was built on the property. It was tasteful and archi-tecturally ingenious, blending with the landscape in a way that showed the owner's love of the land.

Lara surreptitiously watched the creation of that house with a sort of weary fascination. It was the house they'd envisioned time and again eight years earlier as they had sat by the stream dreaming of the future. They had planned each room with such care, imagined the views and even the furniture and, most of all, the laughter that would fill the house. It had been a wonderful dream, woven by lovers ensnared by threads of magic.

The reality was a torment, mocking testimony to her failure to keep her father's legacy intact. Worse, it was a painful daily reminder of a past she should have forgotten, but hadn't. The anguish that house represented might have broken a lesser woman. It gave Lara Danvers a reason to fight.

One

The house—Steven's house—had been empty for weeks now, and Lara had finally begun to relax. She had no idea where he'd gone this time, but she was grateful for the reprieve. There had been no unexpected, disturbing glimpses of him fishing in the creek, faded cutoff jeans riding low on his hips, his bare shoulders burnished by the sun. Nor had there been any awkward chance encounters in town, those heart-stopping moments when their gazes would clash and all the passion and anguish would flare to life like tinder touched by a dangerous spark.

The last few years had been made unbearable by such incidents. The comfort and peace she had finally found in her quiet life on the farm had been shattered in the wink of an eye by a man who shouldn't have mattered at all. During those increasingly erratic times he was in residence, simply walking at twilight on her own land or stopping at Beaumont's for a soda no longer brought the simplest pleasure or anticipation. Her heart thundered with dread each time she rounded a bend in the stream. Her pulse raced when she caught a glimpse of sun-streaked brown hair or even the flash of blue and chrome on a pickup through the drugstore window.

Trust had died. Why not the love? Why not this stirring of her blood at the mention of his name? Why not the yearning ache that had settled around her heart? After all this time, shouldn't they be gone as well?

For a while she'd deluded herself that anger was responsible for the intensity of her responses, but on days she was being honest she admitted it was something very different. Fate had seemingly decreed that Steven would be the unforgettable passion of her life. Try as she might, she'd never been able to replace the excitement he'd brought into her previously tame world with his intelligence and vitality and laughter.

The early-morning chores done, Lara sat on the porch and watched the night's veil of darkness lift, giving way to the first gray hint of dawn. This was her favorite time of day, the quiet moments that were hers alone. The last of yesterday's rain clouds drifted away. Streaks of pink came next, lazily over the horizon. Then a wash of gold and a blaze of orange. The beauty of it kept other, pointless thoughts at bay for a time.

Considering her odd mood of late, it was good that Tommy had left the children with her for the summer, while he and Megan resettled in Kansas City.

Jennifer and Kelly were a handful, giving her little time to dwell on other things. Their fascination with everything from butterflies to tractors filled the days with endless questions and childish laughter. Lara always felt better when they were around, stronger, happier. They filled the empty spaces in her life in a way that all the hard work and success with the farm had been unable to do.

Perhaps later in the morning they could go down to the stream. With Steven away again and not even his housekeeper around to catch them, it would be safe enough, and the weather promised to be perfect for a picnic. It would be a special treat for all three of them. Something to distract her inquisitive, restless nieces, a reminder of her own distant childhood for her.

As busy as the farm had been in summer, her father had always found at least one morning to wake her and her brothers at dawn for a day of fishing. Adoring him as she had, it had been the highlight of her summer. It had been a time to throw aside cares, to splash in the cool water and be children for once.

There had been ice cold lemonade in a huge yellow and white Thermos, thick peanut-butter-and-jelly sandwiches and oatmeal cookies sweet with raisins. The competition to catch the biggest fish had been intense, yet there had been so much laughter and teasing that victor and losers had been equally content.

At the end of the day they'd proudly carried home their string of fish for mama to fry for dinner. Every year she'd said the exact same thing, as they'd waited expectantly for her to lift the first forkful to her mouth.

"I declare this is just about the best fish I ever did eat," she'd say, and smiles would widen. "You children must know just the right spot in that stream."

Lara had always agreed with her. Each year it had been the best fish ever, the flavor of last year's dimmed by time, the taste of this year's heightened by excitement.

Now, her plans for the day made, she went back into the kitchen, poured herself another cup of coffee and set about packing the picnic. She was just finishing up when Jennifer and Kelly padded softly into the kitchen, their cheeks flushed, their blond hair in curly disarray. Kelly, thumb poked in her mouth, came to Lara's side and leaned against her leg, waiting patiently to be picked up. Morning was about the only time of day that Kelly was docile.

Lara scooped the affectionate two-year-old into her arms and plucked the thumb from her mouth. "If you keep sucking on that thumb, it's going to fall off one day," she teased.

"It will not," Jennifer said. "That's what Daddy always told me, too, but mine never did. See." She held out her hands.

Lara examined both thumbs solemnly. "Yes, indeed. You must be one of the lucky ones. But how would you feel, if Kelly weren't so lucky? Now why don't I give you both some pancakes for breakfast. Wouldn't that be much better than any old thumb?"

Kelly nodded happily and, fully awake now, squirmed to get down. Jennifer gazed at Lara with a wise, unblinking stare. It was clear that she'd recognized the bribe for what it was. It was just as obvious that her desire for pancakes outweighed her sense of duty to keep her sister informed of adult wiles.

When both girls were settled at the table with breakfast in front of them, Lara told them about the surprise she'd planned.

"Picnic," Kelly repeated, waving a forkful of syrupy pancakes excitedly. Lara patiently redirected the food to her mouth. She always considered it a coup if more than half a meal actually made its way to the child's stomach.

"I thought you didn't like us to go to the river," Jennifer said.

"I don't usually, but this is a special occasion."

"And we can go swimming?"

"If the water's warm enough."

"Do we have to go fishing?"

"Don't you want to?"

Jennifer shook her head adamantly.

"Have you ever been?"

"Don't you remember, Aunt Lara? Daddy took me once. He had these yucky worms, and he stuck a big hook into them. It made me sick."

Lara hid her grin, recalling Tommy's bemusement at Jennifer's disgust. "Now I remember. You don't have to touch the worms if you don't want to, but wouldn't it be fun to catch a big fish and fix it for dinner tonight?"

Jennifer, who had her father's solemn, thoughtful personality if not his love of fishing, pondered that seriously. "Maybe."

Disappointed, Lara decided that was the best she could hope for. So what if the girls didn't fish. They could swim. It wouldn't spoil her day. Nothing was going to ruin this chance to bring back old memories.

An hour later the girls were dressed in their swimsuits, and the three of them were walking through the woods. Sunlight shimmered through the leaves, creating a patchwork of shades of green. The grass was cool and damp, the sun warm. The air was filled with that heavy, earthy scent of a forest recently bathed by rain. It was normally a short walk, lengthened today by excited explorations. There were wildflowers to be identified, squirrels to chase and birds to watch.

"What's this?" Kelly asked, yanking a flower up by its roots for perhaps the tenth time since they'd started out.

"A buttercup."

"Everybody knows that," Jennifer said with all the smugness of her advanced years.

"Okay, Miss Smarty-pants," Lara said to her. "You show us which way north is."

Jennifer stood still and looked around, her mouth drawn down in a thoughtful frown. Then her eyes lit up. "This way." She pointed in the right direction.

"What makes you think so?"

"Because Daddy told me to look for moss on the back of the trees."

Lara ruffled Jennifer's curls. "What am I going to do with you? Pretty soon you're going to be smarter than me."

"Then I'll tell you things," Jennifer promised.

"I want to swim," Kelly said, clearly tired of her sister's display of learning. "Want to swim now!"

Lara took her hand. If Jennifer was the quiet, patient, stubborn one, Kelly was all impulsiveness and unbridled enthusiasm. Jennifer could spend hours alone with a book. Kelly preferred blocks she could stack into lopsided towers or a swing that could carry her high enough to touch an oak tree's lowest branches. Lara could imagine Jennifer growing up to be a research scientist, while Kelly was just as likely to be a sky diver. How had Tommy and Megan produced children with two such different personalities?

"Then let's get moving," Lara said, responding to Kelly's demand for action. "First one into the stream wins what?"

"An extra cookie," Jennifer shouted.

"Okay. Go!"

They heard the rush of water before they saw it. Then suddenly the stream's surface sparkled before them. Jennifer squealed with delight and ran to the edge, putting one foot cautiously in to test the temperature before plunging ahead to claim her prize for being first. With no hesitation at all, Kelly toddled right in behind her on plump, sturdy legs. Within minutes they were happily splashing in the shallow water, no doubt scaring away the fish, Lara decided with regret.

As the girls played, she spread out the blanket, opened the picnic hamper and set out the things for lunch. She read for a while, then took off the T-shirt she'd worn over her bathing suit and walked down to join them at the water's edge.

"This is fun, Aunt Lara. Nobody's here. I don't see why we can't come all the time," Jennifer said, splashing water on her. Lara shivered as the cool drops hit her warm flesh, but it was Jennifer's innocent request that really chilled her.

"We just can't."

"But why not?"

Frustration and tension began to build, along with a renewed sense of loss. This should still be Danvers land, she thought with familiar bitterness. It should never have fallen into the hands of a stranger. Steven, though she'd known him intimately, in the end had been little more than a stranger, a man it seemed she'd never really known at all. Each month she put away money to buy back the land someday, but the goal was a long way off, and she had no way of knowing if she could even convince Steven to sell.

"Aunt Lara, why can't we come all the time?" Jennifer persisted.

"Yes. Why not?" a deceptively soft and very masculine voice inquired. Lara's head snapped around. It was as if by thinking of Steven, she'd conjured him up. She fought the desire to wrap herself in a towel to hide her swimsuit-clad body from his piercing eyes.

"You—" she began in confusion, her heart pounding. "I thought you were away."

"I'm sure you did," Steven said, an unmistakable wry note in his voice. "Otherwise, I'm sure you wouldn't be here."

Taken by surprise, Lara found herself caught between the fury she'd nurtured for so long and an instinctive reawakening of desire. She was helpless to stop the rush of her blood, the hammering of her heart. She could hardly tear her gaze away from the man who stood before her. His eyes were the same shade of vivid blue she'd remembered, his smile every bit as devastating. Only a scattering of gray hairs in the darker curls on his chest hinted of the years that had passed since they'd been in this very spot together. Like the tide responding to the moon, she felt herself drawn to him as she had been then.

"We'll leave," she said, determinedly turning her back on him to hide the hard thrust of her aroused and swollen breasts. She began to gather the picnic things she had just spread out.

Steven took the loaded hamper from her shaking hands and put it back down. "Are you so afraid of me?" he asked, his eyes on the shallow rise and fall of her chest, his voice lowered to a pitch that wouldn't carry to the girls.

Her chin lifted, but she couldn't meet his gaze. "I am not afraid of you, but this is your land now. We're trespassing."

"Lara, don't you think you're carrying this feud too far?" he said with a touch of impatience. "Go back into the water, then finish your picnic. Let the girls enjoy themselves. You're always welcome here."

"Will you leave then?" The question was bold and rude, but necessary.

His lips curved in a faint smile. "Like you said, it's my land."

The arrogance of the response was exactly what she might have expected. If she'd hoped for a change after all these years, there was her proof that change in such a man was impossible. She was welcome here, but only if she accepted his presence as well. It was no deal at all.

"Who are you?" Jennifer suddenly inquired. Dripping wet and shivering, she and Kelly were standing right beside Steven. Lara quickly bent to wrap them both in towels.

He stooped down to their height and introduced himself. "I'm Steven Drake. Who are you?"

"I'm Jennifer Danvers, and this is my sister, Kelly. That's my Aunt Lara. Do you know her?"

He cast a meaningful sideways glance at Lara. "I've known her for a very long time."

"Too long," Lara muttered.

Steven ignored her. Deliberately focusing his attention on her nieces, he said, "I see a fishing rod, but I don't see any fish around here. Didn't you catch any?"

"Fishing's yucky," Jennifer declared.

"Yucky," Kelly echoed.

"Then you must not be doing it right," he said. "How about if I show you what to do?"

He picked up Lara's fishing rod and, before she could protest, walked a little way upstream with it. Without so much as a glance for permission, the girls followed him as if he were some sort of pied piper. She watched their sudden fascination with hooks and worms with a growing sense of irritation. Not only had he deftly blocked her escape, he was now setting out to win over her nieces, and from what she could see, he was doing an effective job of it. She should have insisted on leaving. Whatever their personal differences, not even at his most insensitive would Steven have been likely to create a scene in front of the children.

Their laughter carried back to her on the still air. Lara suffered a sharp pang of something she could only label jealousy. Dear God, how easily he'd fit in. How natural he was with Jennifer and Kelly, as if entertaining small children were something he did often and enjoyed. It reminded her all too clearly of other times right here, times when they'd talked of having a family of their own. She'd been able to envision Steven's children as clearly then as if they'd been real—the boy a miniature of the handsome father, all laughing charm and athletic grace; the daughter, bold and beautiful and vital.

A loud squeal of delight suddenly broke into her thoughts.

"Aunt Lara, come quick! I caught a fish!" Jennifer's excitement was mirrored by Kelly's. Both of the girls were clapping their hands together and jumping up and down. Steven was watching them with tolerant amusement as he removed the three inch fish from the hook.

"Can we have it for dinner tonight?" Jennifer begged.

Lara exchanged a look with Steven. "Honey, it's pretty small," he said. "It wouldn't be much more than a mouthful. Maybe you should let it go so it can grow up to be a great big fish."

Jennifer looked at her prize catch thoughtfully. "He is little," she admitted. "What should I do, Aunt Lara?"

"That's up to you, but I think maybe Mr. Drake is right. He's just a baby. By next summer he'd be plenty big, and you could try to catch him again."

Jennifer took the tiny, squirming fish by its tail and squinted into its left eye. "Okay," she said finally, as if satisfied by the exchange. She took a few steps into the water and lowered the fish gently into the stream.

"Bye, fish," she said solemnly as she let it go.

Kelly, her expression clouding over, poked her thumb into her mouth.

"All this talk of fish has made me very hungry. How about some lunch?" Lara suggested as a distraction.

"Mr. Drake, too?" Jennifer asked.

"I'm sure Mr. Drake has things to do this afternoon."

"Nothing that can't wait," he said, meeting her gaze evenly, the challenge clear.

"He can share my sandwich," Jennifer offered as a convincing final argument.

Lara sighed and gave in to the inevitable. She distributed the peanut-butter-and-jelly sandwiches and lemonade, carefully avoiding all eye contact with Steven. The first bite of her sandwich seemed to lodge in her throat and stay there. She had no appetite for more.

Suddenly warm fingers brushed hers as Steven took the sandwich from her hand. "If you're not going to finish that, I will," he said.

"Steven," she began impatiently, then got lost in the expression in his eyes. How many times had he stolen the last bite of her sandwich, the last cookie, the last swallow of her drink? It had been a running joke that she'd have to learn to eat faster or starve to death around him. He grinned boldly, and she knew he was remembering, too. The gesture had been a deliberate taunt.

"We have to go," she said, hurriedly cleaning up the debris from lunch. "It's time for the girls' nap."

"They're already half-asleep now," he pointed out. "Why disturb them?"

"Their bathing suits are wet. They could get a chill." It was the best excuse she could come up with, far better than admitting that she was the one who wanted to leave.

"Lara, it's eighty-five degrees out here. They're not going to get a chill."

"But they're in the shade."

"Lara." Amusement filled his voice. "Would it be so terrible to spend just a little time with me? We have a lot to catch up on."

"I have nothing to say to you," she insisted.

That drew a grin that sent a tingle down her spine. "Oh, I doubt that. I think you have quite a bit to say. What about all those things you didn't get to say eleven years ago? Or maybe what you wanted to tell me that day in the bank when I bought this land? Start there and we can work our way up to the present."

"I try not to use that sort of language in front of the girls."

He threw back his head and laughed at her deliberately prim tone. Ironically, Lara found herself wanting to laugh with him, wanting to put all the pain and anger behind as if it had never been.

Apparently he sensed her confusion, because he pressed his advantage. "Don't you think we could be friends again, if we tried?"

Friends? It was such a pale word for the way she'd once thought of him. Soul mate was closer. Lover even more accurate. But it had started with friendship. Did she dare allow it to start like that again, when she knew the feelings that still stirred inside her at the sight of him?

"I think that would be a mistake," she said at last. "Wasn't it some ancient philosopher who once said that 'even God cannot change the past'?"

"I don't want to change it. I just want us both to learn to live with it."

"I've lived with it every day for the past eleven years. I don't need you reminding me of it." She'd blurted the words out angrily, without thinking of the implication of her admission.

He sighed. He reached out a hand to touch her, but she jerked away. "Oh, Lara, did I hurt you so badly? I'm sorry. I never meant to do that."

Blinded by sudden tears and determined that he wouldn't see them, she got to her feet. "It's far too late for being sorry, Steven, and I certainly don't need any sympathy from you. Just go on with your life, and let me go on with mine."

He stood beside her. Before she realized his intention this time, he was tracing the line of her jaw with his finger. She felt the shock of that touch ricocheting through her.

"I don't think I can do that, sweetheart. Not anymore." There was an apologetic note in his voice, but the gleam of determination glowed in his eyes. She knew that look all too well, and it made her quake inside.

"You have to," she said, her words edged with quiet desperation. She swore it was the closest she would ever come to a plea. Even before he responded, she could see from his expression that he intended to ignore it.

"Sorry."

Lara could take no more. "Jennifer! Kelly! Wake up, girls. It's time to go home."

They were slow, impossibly slow, and each second they took to wake and get ready to leave made her hands shake and her nerves stretch taut. Steven seemed to regard her mounting anxiety with lazy fascination, which only added to her sense of being caught like a rabbit in a snare, heart fluttering with fear.

Without saying another word, he watched her as she led the girls off toward the path through the woods. She could feel his gaze on her and wondered at the wistfulness she'd seen pass quickly across his rugged features. Then she thought of the strong resolution that had replaced it in his eyes, and she shivered, only barely resisting the impulse to run. She knew instinctively that he would not give up so easily. He never had. Steven was a man who set clear goals for himself and attained them with dogged determination. Her escape today had merely been a brief reprieve.

Two

The white frame house was bathed in moonlight. Steven stood staring at it for the longest time, as if willing a light to go on in Lara's upstairs window. The relentless darkness mocked him, effectively shutting him out.

It had been years since he'd done this, years since he'd waited outside like a lovesick teenager hoping for a glimpse of a girl who'd caught his fancy. Even though he'd been twenty-seven back then, that's the way he'd felt from the moment he'd laid eyes on Lara Danvers down at the stream.

It had been a hot, dry summer day. A Thursday, he recalled, because his weekly meeting with his accountant to go over the books had been cancelled at the last minute. He'd decided to take advantage of the unexpected free time and explore the area. He'd even planned to take a swim to cool off, if he could find a deserted spot along the stream that edged much of the farmland he was interested in buying.

He'd driven along a dusty dirt road for several miles, then abandoned his car and walked through a stretch of woods. When he'd come upon the stream, dappled by sunlight, it had been irresistible. Seeing no one around, he'd stripped off his clothes and waded in, the cool water a welcome shock to his heated flesh.

That's when he'd seen her.

She was emerging from the woods maybe a hundred yards downstream. Her hair, the longest he'd ever seen, hung down her back in a shimmering wave. It glistened in the sunlight like tangled threads of purest gold. Her face was that of a Viking maiden, its structure and her coloring more than adequate hints of her Scandinavian ancestry. She was tall, her slender and tanned legs extended from hips that curved enticingly. She moved with an easy, unselfconscious grace, totally unaware of the tempting picture she presented.

She had bent down to remove her shoes, then curled her toes into the cool grass. Then she'd flung out her arms, as if to embrace the world, her face turned up to catch the sun. Steven's breath had caught in his throat and he'd waited, God help him, to see what would happen next. Would blouse and shorts follow the shoes? Would she join him in the water in naked abandon? He felt as though he'd stumbled into the Garden of Eden, caught between innocence and sensuality.

Still clothed, she had waded into the water to her knees, laughing like a child. He thought he'd never seen a woman so beautiful or heard a sound so delightful.

Perhaps if she hadn't been moving directly toward him, he would have kept his silence and carried the memory away like a rare and special dream. But she kept getting closer, and enchanted as he was, he hadn't wanted to cause her any embarrassment. He'd finally spoken, his voice a husky whisper, lacking its usual self-confidence.

"Hello."

Startled, she'd turned at the sound. She stared at him, and he'd seen then that her eyes were an amazing shade of gray-blue, like the morning sea touched with a fading beam of moonlight. He also realized for the first time that she was young. Though there were strength and maturity in her face, he guessed she was still in her teens, certainly no more than twenty.

She'd glanced along the shore then and seen his hastily discarded clothes. Instead of embarrassment, a teasing smile had flashed across her face.

"I don't suppose you want to come ashore so we can have a proper introduction," she said.

He'd frowned with feigned severity. "You know perfectly well if I come ashore right now, there would be nothing proper about it."

She'd laughed at that, a sparkling, clear sound. "Don't scold me. You're the one skinny-dipping in my stream."

That's how it had begun, amid taunts and laughter and smoldering sensuality. He'd tried to stay away from her, especially after he'd learned she was only eighteen. But even at that age, Lara was a lady not easily ignored. Experienced as he was at evading the tender wiles of women, he'd been no match for her total lack of guile. With a touch both innocent and captivating, she'd lured him onto what he'd thought was no more than a merry-go-round of mild flirtation, only to discover it was as wild as any roller-coaster ride he'd ever taken. She'd been mysterious and elusive, eager and bold by turns. Never knowing what to expect, he'd awakened each day with a glorious sense of anticipation.

In time, though, it had had to end, but the leaving had been painful, worse than any he'd ever experienced before. Now here he was back again, risking the same emotional maelstrom. He took the package he'd brought to the back porch and left it in the same place he'd left other gifts before.

With a last wry glance in the direction of the house, he set off for home, hoping he wouldn't have cause to regret the gesture. Though she'd seemed tamer somehow today, the spirited Lara he remembered so well was quite capable of throwing it right back in his face.

Thump!

A fine mist of flour filled the air as Lara slammed the bread dough down on the kitchen counter. She flattened the dough, folded it over and pounded it with her fist until her arm was worn-out from the effort. She took a deep breath, briefly enjoying the scent of yeast combined with that of the roses she'd brought in earlier from the garden. Then she picked up the dough and flung it down again. It landed with another satisfying thud.

"That man," she muttered under her breath as she aimed another fierce blow at the soft center of the lump. "How dare he, after all this time? Who does he think he is? I have half a mind to go over there—"

"What man, Aunt Lara?" Jennifer asked.

Startled, Lara gazed blankly at her niece, who had crept into the room and was staring at her with those wide, solemn eyes that were so like Tommy's. Jennifer had a disconcerting way of sneaking up on her. Lara had never seen a child who could move so quietly or remain so still. Nor had she ever met one at that age who was quite so astute.

"How long have you been standing there, little one?"

"I don't know," she said, then with single-minded purpose repeated, "What man, Aunt Lara? Where are you going? Can Kelly and me go, too?"

"Kelly and I," she corrected automatically.

Jennifer apparently heard the unintentionally sharp note that lingered in her voice and regarded her wisely. "Are you mad at someone?"

Lara sighed. "Not really," she said, unable to think of a logical way to explain that she was always mad at one particular man. It didn't take any overt act on Steven Drake's part to infuriate her. His mere existence was irritation enough.

His behavior yesterday had been infuriating enough, but today he'd fueled her ire by leaving a basket of strawberries on the back steps. She'd practically tripped over them when she'd gone out at dawn to milk the two cows she still kept in the barn. There had been no note in the basket, but she'd known at once who the luscious, ripe berries were from. When they'd first met, Steven had made a habit of making such unexpected, romantic little gestures. They'd had the desired effect on an impressionable eighteen-year-old, but now she was beyond such blatant attempts to charm.

Back then in the summer, it was always strawberries or her favorite cherry tomatoes or a bouquet of wildflowers. In the fall it had been a pumpkin, a crooked smile and laughing eyes already carved on its broad orange face. In winter there had been fragrant pine boughs at Christmas, even a soft woolen scarf in a shade of blue he knew was her favorite. By spring he'd been gone, taking joy and hope and love with him. Today's strawberries, no matter how sweet, had been a bitter reminder of the tender courtship that had led nowhere.

"Can I help make the bread?" Jennifer asked now, interrupting the disturbing memories.

Welcoming the prospect of her niece's distracting companionship, she said, "Sure. Climb on up on this stool."

She broke off a chunk of dough and showed Jennifer what to do. Soon they were both pounding happily away, sending puffs of flour into the air. It would take her the rest of the afternoon to clean the floor, Lara thought, then dismissed her dismay. It was worth it. She was never more contented than she was in the kitchen. There was something about baking especially that soothed her. She might even make a strawberry pie, when the bread was finished. There was no point in letting those blasted berries go to waste.

"Something smells wonderful in here," a deep, lazy voice drawled from just the other side of the screened door.

Lara's breath caught in her throat. To her regret, she'd heard the echoes of that voice a million times in her dreams. Now it was all too real. Why? Why after all this time would Steven come here? Yesterday she'd been on his land, their meeting accidental, but this was a blatant invasion of the sanctity of her home. Her fingers dug into the soft dough.

"What are you doing here?" Her voice was as cold and unwelcoming as she could make it, though a wicked flame seemed to heat her blood.

The screen door squeaked on its hinges as it opened and closed. Still, she refused to turn around. She didn't move at all.

"Hi! We're making bread," Jennifer informed him, clearly thrilled by his appearance. "Aunt Lara makes the best bread in the whole world."

"I'll bet she does."

"You want to help?"

"I think I'll just watch."

Lara glanced at him at last, fighting against the shock of looking into his eyes. Those eyes of his had always been her undoing. A vivid blue, they had seemed able to see into her soul. Whatever secrets she'd kept from others had never been hidden to Steven's searching gaze. She wondered if he could sense her confusion now. She wanted him out of her kitchen, but she didn't want Jennifer to witness the fireworks likely to result from her request that he leave at once.

"I think I hear Kelly stirring," she said to Jennifer. "Why don't you go check on her?"

"I didn't hear anything."

"Jennifer!"

Her lower lip curved into a pout. "Okay." Then Jennifer offered Steven her sunniest smile. "Will you still be here when I come back?"

"I hope so." There was a dry note to his voice that Lara couldn't miss.

"I'll hurry then," she promised as she ran from the room. "We hardly ever have company."

"Cute girl," he said, when they were alone. "Is it true what she said?"

"What?"

"That you never have company?"

"I don't see that that's any of your business."

Steven shrugged, plucked a strawberry from the basket he'd left and bit into it. Lara had to force herself not to watch as he licked the red juice from his lips. She wanted to tell him to get out, but now that she'd created the opportunity to say the words, they wouldn't come.

"You didn't say yesterday. Is she Tommy's?"

Lara nodded. "His oldest. She and Kelly are staying here for the summer."

When he said nothing, she felt an urgent need to fill the silence. "Tommy's doing very well. He's just gotten a job with a big firm in Kansas City. He and Megan are there now, looking for a house. The girls will be going out there in the fall. I'll miss them terribly, and it's been good to have them here. They love the farm. It's not like it was when I was growing up. We

have help around here now, so I have time to spend
with them. They're at that age where everything fas-
cinates them. The days don't seem long enough to
show them everything."

She caught herself rambling and suddenly fell silent. Steven leaned back against the counter, crossed
his jeans-clad legs at the ankles and watched her. Agi-
tated, she worked the dough even harder. At the rate
things were going, it would be very tough bread.

"You still haven't said what you wanted," she said
at last.

"Nothing special. Just a neighborly visit."

Her gaze rose and met his, caught the knowing
gleam in his eyes. "Neighbors don't usually wait for
years before dropping in."

"Would I have been welcome any sooner?"

"You're not welcome now."

"I'd hoped—"

"What? That the strawberries would soften me up."

He grinned. "Well, you are harder than you used to
be," he admitted. "I could see that yesterday. It might
take more than strawberries, but I figured that would
be a start. I've been waiting all this time for some sign
that you're ready to let go of the past, but you won't
even look at me when we pass on the street in town."

The dough hit the counter with a resounding thud.
"Did you honestly expect me to greet you with open
arms?" The angry words were out before she could
stop them, yet another admission of a pain she hadn't
wanted him to see. Where was her Danvers' pride?

"No, not open arms." His voice went quiet, and the hint of laughter left it for once. That softening shook her. "Just an open mind."

Lara felt a sigh ripple through her.

"What's happened to you, Lara? When we met, you were filled with so much gaiety, so much excitement. I'll never forget that day I first saw you down at the stream."

"I've grown up a lot since then."

"Growing up shouldn't mean an end to laughter. I've watched you over the last few years. You never seem to laugh anymore. It's as though someone broke your spirit. Was it me?"

The observation rankled. "I hate to spoil your egotistical fantasy that you've ruined my life, but I'm quite happy. I have a full life—family, friends, work."

"That's not what I hear. I hear the only thing in your life is this farm."

"Gossip is a pretty unreliable source of information."

"It's all I've had, since you've made it plain you don't want me around."

"I'm surprised you bothered even with that."

"I wanted to know how you were doing."

"Why? So you could buy up the rest of the farm the minute it fails? I hate to disappoint you, but we're operating in the black."

"I know that, too."

Lara stared at him, incredulous that he'd apparently been prying into her life. "Mr. Hogan, I suppose?"

"He's very proud of your success."

"He's glad the bills are being paid," she retorted with a touch of asperity. Forcing a more cheerful tone, she said, "Well, now that you've seen for yourself how terrific things are around here, you can be on your way."

Steven ignored the blatant dismissal. "You've never married."

Lara's hands stilled. "So? Marriages don't guarantee happiness. From everything you had told me about yours, you of all people should know that."

He winced. "You're right. I was just a kid, and my marriage wasn't a particularly happy one. That doesn't mean I wouldn't try again, if the right woman came along. What about you?"

"I suppose, if the right man came along, I'd marry."

"But in all these years he hasn't appeared? Maybe your standards are impossibly high."

She frowned at the sarcasm. She'd heard the same thing from Tommy all too often. Even mild-mannered Megan chastised her for shutting herself away on the farm. Only Greg, the youngest of the three siblings, left her alone. He was too absorbed with his paintings to even notice the rest of the family. Choosing a solitary existence for himself, he saw nothing odd about her life-style.

Her resentment of the familiar refrain was all too clear in her tone. "Your mythical perfect woman apparently hasn't shown up, either, or am I wrong?" she said, attempting to turn the tables and put him on the defensive. "Have there been other women since you left here eleven years ago?"

"There've been women," he admitted curtly.

"But no marriages?"

"No. I think I was spoiled."

"Oh?" She heard a note in his voice that puzzled her. It was the same solemn hint of regret she'd caught at the bank the day he'd offered to buy her land.

He picked up a small piece of dough, worked it nervously for several minutes as tension built. The air was still, crackling with the promise of a storm and something more. At last he dropped the dough back onto the counter and let his hands fall to his sides.

"I've missed you, Lara."

Her eyes widened in shock. That disconcerting quiet note was back in his voice. He actually sounded sincere. "What did you say?"

"I've missed you," he repeated with a touch of belligerence. "Is that so hard to believe?"

"Since you're the one who walked out on me without a word, yes, it is a little surprising."

"We all make mistakes."

"And I was one of yours?"

"Not you, Lara. Leaving you. That was the mistake. At the time I was so sure it was the right thing to do, but now I don't know."

She swallowed hard. "I think you'd better go."

"Nope," he said, his voice merely conversational rather than challenging. "I ran away once before. I won't do it again, not without explaining, not without trying to make things right."

"How can I get through to you? I don't want your strawberries or your explanations. I don't want to have casual little chats with you about old times. In fact, I don't want you here at all." Her voice rose, ending on a note of frustration.

"I think you do." He took a step closer. "I think that's why your cheeks are flushed that becoming shade of pink and your pulse is racing."

"If my cheeks are flushed, it's because I'm angry," she retorted. "And my pulse is not racing."

A rough, tanned finger reached out, and she jerked away instinctively, backing up. He pursued her. A single step was all it took. He touched her neck gently, found the telltale pulse and lingered for just an instant. "Liar," he said.

Furious and suddenly all too vulnerable, Lara felt tears form in her eyes. "Why are you doing this?"

"Because I've waited long enough."

"Long enough for what?"

"For you to come to your senses. Long enough to see if I was right."

"Right about what?"

"I came back here three years ago hoping that I'd been wrong, praying that you weren't the reason no other woman appealed to me. I had this image of you in my mind that wouldn't go away. It was there when I was awake. It was there when I slept. Worse, it was there no matter whom I held in my arms."

His gaze met hers, and she saw the shadow of pain in his eyes. It stunned her that Steven had not escaped the past years without scars, either. She tried to steel herself against what she saw. It made him appear defenseless, more accessible than the heartless man who'd been able to distance himself from a girl he'd promised to love. His smile now was a weary hint of the blaze of pleasure it had once been.

"Then I saw you," he said, sounding as bemused as she felt. "God, how you'd changed. There were shadows under your eyes. You'd pulled that incredible golden hair of yours back so severely that all I wanted to do was yank it loose and run my fingers through it until it was the wild tangle I'd remembered. And you were thin, all those ripe adolescent curves gone. But I wanted you, just the same. I wanted you so badly I hurt, just the way my body is hurting right now. I knew right then that I could never let you go again."

"Stop it," she pleaded. "Stop saying that. You left, Steven. You betrayed me. You betrayed all of us. You can never change that. It's too late. I don't want you back."

As if her words had been a challenge, a slow, gentle smile, brighter now, tugged at the corners of his lips. "I'll make you want me again, Lara. You know I can do it, too, don't you?"

His words were spoken confidently, laced with a dare. Once Lara might have taken him up on it, but no more. She'd built a quiet, pleasant life for herself. Safe. More secure than ever, now that the farm was doing well each year. Steven Drake would not waltz in here one summer afternoon and take that hard-won serenity away from her.

Oh, but he has, she thought. That's exactly what he's done. If he left right now and never came back, he would take her hard-won peace of mind with him.

"You're still here!" Jennifer shouted with enthusiasm as she came back into the kitchen, tugging Kelly with her. The two-year-old's eyes were still sleepy, and she held her favorite blanket clutched in one hand. The end was dragging on the floor. "Kelly's just a baby. She still has to take a nap."

Steven reached down and scooped Kelly up. She promptly put her head on his shoulder. Lara glared at her.

"She doesn't look like a baby to me," he said. His voice was filled with such tenderness and delight that it tugged at Lara's heart. It was as if he'd guessed that the free-spirited, independent Kelly was closest to the way Lara had once been. Did he recognize the similarity she'd felt so often and responded to it as she did?

"I think she's almost as pretty as you are," he said to Jennifer.

"You think I'm pretty?" Jennifer asked, twirling around excitedly.

"Absolutely. When you grow up, I'll bet you'll be as beautiful as your Aunt Lara." His eyes met Lara's, but she looked away, unable to deal with the clear message she saw there.

"Tell you what, girls," he was saying now, his voice so deliberately casual, he immediately aroused Lara's suspicion. "Why don't you come over and go swimming again tomorrow? I have it on good authority that there are bigger fish waiting to be caught, too."

Jennifer's eyes lit up. Even Kelly, normally slow to wake fully from her naps, seemed to perk up at the prospect of another adventure.

"Oh, can we, Aunt Lara?" Jennifer begged. "Swimming's the most fun of anything, and I want to catch that big fish before Kelly and me have to go away."

Helpless in the face of their enthusiasm, Lara evaded giving a direct response. "We'll see."

"Noon?" Steven persisted. "This time I'll have my housekeeper fix the picnic."

Another picnic by the stream with its inevitable memories was the very last thing Lara intended to do with Steven. He'd reached new heights of insensitivity just by suggesting such a thing. Then, clearly aware of her discomfort, he'd knowingly backed her even further into a corner. The man was maddening.

"I don't think so," she said finally. "It would be too much trouble, and we have things to do tomorrow, anyway."

"What things?" he and Jennifer said in a chorus.

She gritted her teeth to keep from yelling. "This is a farm. There are always things to do."

"But you said earlier you had enough help now," Steven reminded her. "Surely you could find the time for a picnic."

"Not tomorrow," she said firmly.

Not ever, she thought.

Steven nodded at last, accepting the finality of her decision. "Okay, kids, we'll do it another time. Your Aunt Lara and I will work it out."

"You promise?" Jennifer inquired skeptically, disappointment etched on her face. That expression was almost Lara's undoing.

"Cross my heart," he said as he put Kelly down and headed for the door.

"No go," Kelly protested at once, dropping her beloved blanket and holding up her arms.

"I'll be back, sweetheart. You can count on it."

The promise was addressed to Kelly and Jennifer, but his eyes were on Lara. Deny it or not, now her cheeks were flushed and her fingers trembled, but she refused to look away. It had been years since she'd felt this way, giddy with excitement and filled with the yearning ache of desire. Too many years, she admitted reluctantly and hated herself for the traitorous response.

"He shouldn't have come back," she murmured when he had gone. "He should never have come back."

But he had.

Three

———

Logan Fairchild stood with one dusty boot propped up on the bottom rung of the split-rail fence. He whipped off the sweat and dirt-stained Stetson he'd worn ever since Lara had hired him and wiped a red bandanna across his weathered face.

Everything about Logan, from his deliberately Western attire to his slow talk, bowlegged walk and rough edges, suggested a man who'd grown up with Texas-style ranching. Lara knew for a fact, though, that Logan had been born not thirty miles away in northwestern Ohio some sixty years ago. In all that time the closest he'd ever been to a cowboy was a John Wayne movie, but he lived out his dream nonetheless. He was the best farm manager she'd ever run across, steady, knowledgeable and willing to take orders from a woman—as long as she listened to his advice first.

"This here corn's lookin' mighty good, Ms. Danvers." Brown eyes scanned the fields spread out before them. "It's Fourth of July, and already it's high as an elephant's eye, just like the song says. I told you this hybrid was gonna do right by us. If the weather holds, you'll have your best year yet."

"I hope so, Logan. I used the last of the money we got for selling the land to buy that new equipment. What with that and hiring the extra men last year we barely made ends meet. I don't want this place to start running in the red again. Tommy and Greg will start in on me again about selling. Since Tommy left, they think the farm is too much for me to handle."

"Not with me around, it's not. Don't you worry. We'll do okay, Ms. Danvers," he said. "If the Lord wants us to."

He pulled an ear of corn off the nearest stalk and stripped away the corn silk to reveal plump yellow kernels. He poked a thumbnail into a juicy kernel and apparently found it tender. He nodded in satisfaction. "We ought to start harvesting this field by the end of the week."

"Do you have the men you need?"

"We should be okay."

"If not, pick up some day workers. I don't want the crop going bad because we couldn't get it harvested in time."

"No chance of that," he chided. "I know my business."

She grinned at him. "Probably better than I do, right, Logan?"

"You're pretty good yourself," he conceded grudgingly. "For a woman."

"How did I know you were going to say that?" she said with a resigned shake of her head. "You're an unrepentant male chauvinist."

He hooted at the charge. "Through and through, Ms. Danvers. Through and through. Now get along with you. That parade's starting in town pretty soon, and you don't want those little ones to miss it."

"They're already having their own parade. They've been carrying flags around the house all morning. I left when Jennifer started beating on a pan." Recalling the noise, she shuddered.

Logan reached into his back pocket and pulled out a whistle he'd carved. "Give her this. Maybe it'll go easier on your nerves."

"Thanks, Logan. I'm sure she'll love it. I know I will."

Lara walked slowly back to the house, thinking about this year's crop. She hoped Logan was right about the new corn. This year could be a turning point for her. With a good crop, she'd be able to add to her special account meant to buy back Steven's property. A bad year could be devastating, especially with the pressure from Tommy and Greg. She didn't know why they'd suddenly gotten it into their heads that she should sell the place, but they could both take a flying leap before she'd consider it. Before her agitation could build, she brought herself up short. She wasn't going to think about that today, not with a big holiday celebration waiting in town.

Long before she reached the house, she could hear the girls. As she turned the corner, she saw them waiting impatiently for her on the porch.

"We make music, Aunt Lara," Kelly said, clapping two pan lids together. The makeshift cymbals were accompanied by Jennifer's improvised drum, the bottom of one of Lara's best pots. The performance made up in enthusiasm and volume what it lacked in rhythm and musicality. Lara shuddered again but kept a smile on her face.

"That's very loud music," she said, a comment she was certain they would consider high praise. "As soon as you're finished with your song we can leave for the parade." The pan and lids clattered to the porch. She shook her head. "Nope. They go back inside."

There was much scurrying before they finally reappeared, miniature American flags in hand. Dressed in red-and-white-striped shirts and blue shorts, they made a patriotic pair. Lara pulled her camera out of her pocket. "Let's get a picture of you two to send to Mommy and Daddy. I'll bet they're missing you a whole lot today."

The girls posed reluctantly, clearly more excited about the prospect of the parade. The instant the camera's shutter clicked, they were off to pile into the car. Jennifer had already fastened her seat belt, and Kelly was crawling into her car seat by the time Lara got there.

The downtown streets were already crowded when they arrived a half hour later. They parked a few blocks from Main Street and walked over to find places on the curb, which was already lined with families.

"Me can't see," Kelly protested, trying to wiggle between adult legs.

"Me, either, Aunt Lara."

"We'll walk a little way down and see if we can't find a better place."

"But the parade's already started. I can hear it," Jennifer lamented, tears welling up. "We're going to miss it all."

Suddenly Steven was blocking their path. Catching sight of Jennifer's tears, he was instantly kneeling down in front of her. "What's all this about?"

Blue eyes were turned on him appealingly. "Kelly and me can't see anything. Everybody's too tall."

"Well, we'll just have to fix that, won't we?" His gaze lifted to meet Lara's. She was trapped. Again. His voice dropped a level. "Hello, Lara."

"Steven."

"Mind if I help out my friends here?"

She shrugged. There was no point in objecting. She'd have two hysterical children on her hands if she did.

Steven lifted Kelly and perched her on his shoulders, then took Jennifer's hand. He approached the family in front of them. "Excuse me, folks. Would you mind if the little one here gets up front so she can see?"

They responded automatically to his smile and parted to create a space for Jennifer. She looked back at him. "You, too."

"Nope. That wouldn't be fair. Your Aunt Lara and I are tall enough to stay back here. We'll be right behind you."

Accepting Steven's word without question, Jennifer turned to watch the parade. Kelly was already wide-eyed as the first band came marching past. She waved her flag so enthusiastically it almost caught Steven in the eye. Lara reached out to take it away from her, but Steven intervened, his hand catching hers in mid-reach. "She's okay. No damage done."

Instead of dropping her hand, he used the incident as an excuse to keep it, holding it in the familiar way of two lovers used to such casual intimacy. Lara's head protested the touch, but her body accepted it all too readily. His flesh was warm, his fingers gentle in their command over her senses. It was the touch of a man who knew well the subtleties of seduction. In time, just when Lara's blood was heating, her heart drumming, he released her. She felt instantly bereft and furious because of it.

The last band marched past, and the crowd began to break up, most of the people heading for the square where a barbecue was being held throughout the afternoon, to be followed by games and dancing and fireworks.

When he'd retrieved Jennifer from her spot along the curb, Steven touched a hand to the small of Lara's back to turn her toward the square. "Come on. I'll buy you all some chicken and corn on the cob."

"Really, that's not necessary," Lara protested.

"Of course, it's not necessary. I want to do it." He tendered his most beguiling grin. "You wouldn't want me to spend the rest of the holiday all alone, would you?"

"With the number of available women in this county, you wouldn't be alone more than five minutes, and you know it."

"But I'd rather choose the one I'll spend my time with. Come on, Lara. It's just a barbecue. Your nieces are with us. We'll be chaperoned by the whole town. How dangerous can it be?"

Lara's heart skipped a beat. She was unable to restrain herself from saying, "I seem to recall that eleven years ago the whole town wasn't enough to keep us from getting into trouble."

Warmth filled his eyes. Their glances caught and held. Time—eleven lonely years—vanished. "I wasn't sure you remembered that night."

"How could I not?" she said, unwillingly lost to the memories. "It was a night that changed my life."

"Mine, too," he said very, very softly, and for just an instant she believed him. "Stay, Lara."

Desire tugged at her. "Steven, I can't."

"Can't or won't? Weren't you planning to take the girls to the barbecue before I came along?"

"Yes," she admitted with a sigh.

"Then you can't very well disappointment them, can you?" he pressed.

"Please, Aunt Lara," Jennifer begged. Even Kelly's bright blue eyes watched her hopefully.

Her eyes flashed angrily as the trap tightened around her. "Dammit, Steven—"

He gave a quick, pointed glance at the two wide-eyed children and held up a hand.

"Hey, Nellie, my love," he called to the grey-haired woman who normally worked behind the old-fashioned soda fountain at Beaumont's. Lara noticed that a blush crept up her cheeks at the affectionate greeting he'd been giving her since he and Lara had gone into the drugstore for milk shakes eleven years ago. Apparently not even women over sixty were immune to Steven's considerable charms. Nellie waited for him, not looking one bit surprised to see Lara and her nieces with him.

"Would you mind doing me a tremendous favor?" he asked her. "You'd be saving my life."

"Steven Drake, I'd walk across hot coals for you," she told him, sharing a conspiratorial grin with Lara. "It's a good thing I'm not a few years younger. I'd take that sweet talk of yours seriously, and then we'd both be in a pack of trouble with your young lady here. What do you need?"

"How about taking Jennifer and Kelly on down to the barbecue for me so I can have a few minutes alone with Lara?"

"Steven," Lara protested.

"I don't mind a bit," Nellie said cheerfully. 'How about it, kids? Shall we go find the biggest pieces of fried chicken we can?"

"And ice cream?" Kelly inquired hopefully.

"I'll bet we can find some ice cream, too."

"Thanks, Nellie. You're an angel. We'll catch up with you in a few minutes," Steven promised.

"Take your time and enjoy yourselves. With my grandkids away, it's a real treat to have some little ones along on a day like this."

As soon as the children and Nellie were out of earshot, Lara whirled on Steven. "How dare you? For the past week you've been barging into my life, using those children to get to me. I don't know what you're after, but I wish to hell you'd tell me and then back off."

The more she fumed, the broader Steven's grin grew. "What's wrong with you?" she demanded. "Why are you laughing at me?"

"I'm not laughing," he said, swallowing a chuckle. "It's just that it's been so long since I've seen you this furious."

"Well, if you're perverse enough to think I'm terrific when I'm angry, you're in for the treat of your lifetime because I am boiling mad, Steven Drake."

She began pacing up and down the sidewalk, drawing amused glances. Her blond hair, drawn up in a ponytail, bounced indignantly. She stopped in front of him finally and put her hands on her hips. She glared straight into his eyes. "You are an insufferable, arrogant, rude man, and I've had just about all I intend to take from you."

"That's better," he praised. "Go for it."

"Damn you!" She waved a hand in his face. "This is not some game."

"Closer to therapy, I'd say."

"You traipse back into town, get some ridiculous notion into your head about wanting me back..." The amused glint in his eyes suddenly registered, and his comment sank in. "What do you mean this is closer to therapy?"

"I told you the other day you needed to do all the yelling you didn't get to do eleven years ago. It's time you got your feelings all out in the open so we can deal with them."

His deliberately calm understanding was almost more than she could take. She began pacing again. "Who made you an expert in psychology? I don't want to deal with what happened eleven years ago. I want to talk about what's going on right now. I want to talk about the way you're trying to manipulate me. I won't have it, do you hear me? I won't have you acting all sweet and attentive with my nieces just to get to me. They're little kids. They won't understand when you stop showing up."

"Any more than you did?" His voice was very quiet.

She halted in midstep and turned slowly back to face him. His expression was unreadable, but his message had been crystal clear.

"Okay," she said at last. "You're right. I didn't understand. I still don't, but can't you see I don't care anymore? Right now all I'm concerned about is the way you're using those girls."

"Who says I'm playing up to those kids to get to you? I happen to like children. They always say exactly what's on their mind, unlike some adults I could mention." He stared at her pointedly before adding, "Besides, Megan asked me to look in on them."

Lara couldn't have been more stunned if he'd slapped her. "Megan?"

"I ran into her before she and Tommy left town. She suggested I drop in and check on them. She didn't like the idea of the three of you being all alone over there and since I am the closest neighbor, she asked if I'd mind. Of course, I said I wouldn't. She didn't want me to mention it to you."

What on earth had Megan been thinking of? Lara wondered, then groaned inwardly. That was an easy one. Romantic that she was, Megan had been plotting, hoping that something exactly like this would happen. Lara had never told her the whole story behind her hatred of Steven. Apparently she'd read something into Lara's hostile attitude toward their neighbor and guessed that it hid some other passion.

"We are hardly alone at the farm," she snapped. "Logan is there every day, and we have a whole crew around. So, if that's the only thing that's brought you by, you can consider your duty discharged." Somehow the remark came out sounding more disgruntled than she would have liked. Steven grinned.

"That's not the only reason I'm coming by, as you perfectly well know. Lara, can't we go to the park, sit down under a tree and talk this through? I feel ridiculous having this conversation in the middle of a sidewalk. It's hotter than blazes out here, and you look as though you're ready to bolt at the first opportunity."

"I am. I think we've already said quite enough for one day."

He rolled his eyes. "Obviously reasoning with you is the wrong tactic." He grabbed her hand and started off down the street. Lara had to run to keep up with him.

"I'm not going with you," she muttered, even though she knew how ridiculous the protest sounded when she quite clearly was going with him. He headed straight for a hundred-year-old oak tree in the park, its massive trunk the perfect backrest, its leaves providing welcome shade.

"Sit."

"I'm not some damn puppy you can order around," she replied mutinously.

He shrugged. "Fine. I'll sit."

He lowered himself to the ground, leaned back against the tree and crossed his outstretched legs at the ankle. Since he was still holding tight to her hand, Lara was left bending awkwardly over him. She scowled at him, then sat, staying as far away as his firm handclasp would allow.

"Talk," he suggested.

Her jaw set stubbornly. "You're the one who wanted to talk."

"Okay. I'll put the words in your mouth. Correct me if I get any of this wrong. You're still upset because of what happened eleven years ago. You're convinced that I betrayed you."

"You did."

"I didn't." When she started to protest, he held up his hand. "I can see why you'd think that, but I did what I thought was best."

"Oh, for heaven's sakes, Steven," she said impatiently. "You keep saying that. How could it have been for the best to walk out on me without a word? I was in love with you. We were planning a future together. Or was I the only one doing the planning?"

He sucked in a deep breath and rubbed a thumb across her knuckles. When he finally answered, his voice was so quiet she had to lean closer to hear it. "No, Lara, you weren't the only one making plans. I wanted to be with you more than I'd ever wanted anything in my life."

Tears sprang to her eyes. Her heart felt as though it were breaking all over again. "Then why didn't you stay?"

He sighed heavily, and his expression grew thoughtful as Lara waited for his response. "There were so many reasons, starting with the fact that I wasn't much of a prize back then."

"I thought you were."

"You saw what I wanted you to see. Did you know, for instance, how much I hated my father? It was the only thing that drove me. I wanted to prove I wasn't like him." He gave a rueful laugh. "Instead, I found myself doing exactly the things he'd always done. I put my career above everything else. It was just beginning to go places when we met. I had to travel a lot."

"I knew all that. It didn't matter."

"It did to me. You were only eighteen. Too young to be making a commitment for a lifetime. I was nearly ten years older, and even I wasn't mature enough to handle things right. I'd already had one marriage fail because of my own inability to handle the responsibility of an honest, full-time relationship. I wasn't about to do the same thing to you. Besides, until I showed up, you'd been dreaming about going to college and being a doctor. I wanted you so much,

I kept forgetting about that. Then your parents reminded me.''

She shook her head. "I can't believe my parents would interfere. They knew how much I loved you. They wouldn't have asked you to leave.''

"No, of course not. They just warned me to stop and think very seriously about what I was doing. They pointed out how much I was expecting you to give up. They were afraid that I'd never settle down entirely, that you'd wake up one day and realize I'd made you miss out on the only thing that had ever mattered to you. You would have resented me terribly for that.''

His gaze lifted and lingered on her face. "Remember that last night at the stream?''

"As if it were yesterday," she admitted in a choked voice. "You held me and made love to me and you . . . you cried." There was a note of surprise in her voice at the end. She had forgotten that, forgotten the shock of seeing tears in the eyes of a man she'd thought stronger than anything. "You knew what you meant to do then, didn't you?''

"I knew," he admitted. "And it hurt.''

There were tears in his eyes now as he asked, "Do you remember what we talked about?''

She stared at him in confusion. All she recalled was being enfolded in his arms, the wild excitement that raced through her at his touch.

"You were so excited about your classes," he prompted, and it began coming back to her. "Your grades had come in. Straight A's. You were absolutely certain you'd be able to get through undergraduate school in less than four years. If you kept getting grades like that there was no question you'd be accepted to medical school."

Lara watched him with a puzzled frown. "You seemed so excited for me."

"I was, but I also knew right then that to continue our relationship would be wrong. I'd been planning to ask you that night to leave town with me, but when I saw how bright your future was, how much you wanted that dream, I couldn't ask you to go. I had to let you have your chance."

Lara swallowed hard. "And that's why you didn't say anything? Couldn't you have given me a choice?"

A faint smile pulled at his lips. "I knew you too well, love. I knew how you'd choose. You were impetuous and in love. You'd have gone with me."

"Of course, I would have."

"And it would have been wrong."

"No, dammit," she protested, even as she realized the depth of his sacrifice. "At least I would have had you. Instead, you left, then Papa died. Not so long afterward, Mama died, too. I had to give up any thought of medical school. So, you see, it was all for nothing."

"There was no way to know that that night. I thought I was giving you your dream. It wasn't until I came back three years ago that I discovered it hadn't come true after all. By then your hatred of me ran so deep I didn't think there was any way to change it."

"Why did you come back?"

"For the reason I gave you the other day. I couldn't stay away any longer. If you'd been happy, if you'd been married, I told myself I wouldn't stay, but you weren't. Even if you wouldn't let me back into your life, I felt I had to be here to watch out for you."

"But you never said anything before now. Why?"

"Fear, I suppose. I could see how you'd reacted to my being back, especially since I'd practically forced you to sell me that land. I didn't know how to approach you to change that. Then I was gone a lot. I had a lot of business interests in other states. And in those years I'd been away, I'd had a lot of experience with engineering. I'd been in Mexico during the earthquake. I'd helped with the rescue operation. When similar disasters took place in other countries, I was asked to come and help. I always went. It was easier than staying here and seeing the look of betrayal in your eyes."

Lara drew her knees up to her chest and wrapped her arms around them. She looked at Steven, saw the haunted expression in his eyes. "Could you leave me alone now? I need to think."

Thankfully this time he didn't fight her. He nodded and got to his feet. "I meant every word I said, Lara. You were the most important thing in my life once. You still are. All I'm asking for is a chance to prove that to you."

Then before she could guess his intention, he leaned down and pressed his lips to hers, a touch of silk and fire that caressed her body and set it aflame. As he started to draw away, her fingers threaded through the hair at the nape of his neck. Their eyes met, questioned and knew. Their breath mingled during that instant of separation, and then she drew him to her again, as incapable of denying herself this moment as he had been. The unexpected, gently inquisitive kiss confirmed what she'd already guessed: the passion had never died, it had merely hidden in wait for his return.

When Steven had gone, she put her head down on her knees and let the tears fall freely. So many years lost, time that could never be replaced. His explanation was plausible enough, but did she dare trust a man to whom words came so easily? There was more than just his precipitous departure to answer for. There was the land.

In the past Steven had used the misfortune of many of the local farmers to gain control of hundreds and hundreds of acres. He'd tried to get her family's land as well, and she wasn't at all sure even now that she hadn't once been a pawn in his game.

All he wanted was a chance, he'd said. But giving it to him would be a risk, a dangerous one.

Then she thought of all the years of loneliness that had vanished with a single touch from his gentle fingers and of the desire that had raged at a single kiss. She could fight him, but her own body acted as a weapon against her, making her doubt that she had a prayer of winning.

"I'll give you your chance, Steven," she murmured finally. "But I'll be one formidable enemy if you betray me again."

The rest of the day passed in a haze. She rejoined the others. She ate, though she couldn't have said what. She played games with the girls, unaware of who won. She even danced just once with Steven, her body turning to liquid fire in his arms, though she remembered that in every detail. The sensation both awed and frightened her, and after that dance she ran from it.

At home the girls were so excited they knocked an entire bottle of bubble bath into the tub while Lara was in the bedroom. When she got back, bubbles had overflowed and were creeping toward the hallway. Kelly couldn't find her favorite bear. Jennifer refused to wear her pink pajamas and insisted on wearing the yellow ones Lara had taken downstairs to wash. Three glasses of water each were necessary before they were under the covers. By the time they had settled down for their bedtime story, Lara felt as if she'd plowed an entire field by herself . . . by hand.

"Aunt Lara," Jennifer said sleepily when the story had ended and Kelly's eyes were shut, her thumb tucked in her mouth.

"What, sweetie?"

"Is Mr. Drake your boyfriend?"

The Velveteen Rabbit fell from Lara's hands. "Why on earth would you ask that?"

"I saw him kiss you. That must mean he likes you, right?"

"Sometimes kisses are just between friends."

"Oh."

Lara regarded her curiously. "You sound disappointed."

"I wanted him to like you, the way Daddy likes Mommy."

"Why?"

She snuggled close to Lara and wrapped her arms around her waist. When she spoke, her voice was sad, and her words were muffled against Lara's chest. "So you won't be lonely when me and Kelly go away."

Lara sighed as tears sprang into her eyes. She rocked Jennifer in her arms. "Oh, baby, that's a long time from now. We have the whole summer together."

But despite her brave words, the end of summer seemed closer than ever.

Four

Jennifer Susan Danvers, you get back over here right this instant," Lara called out as Jennifer and Kelly bounded ahead of her to the edge of the woods. "And bring your sister with you."

"Why, Aunt Lara? I want to go to the stream."

"I've told you why. It's not on our land."

"But we went before, and Mr. Drake said it's okay. You heard him." She faced Lara with indignation. "He invited us."

Damn the man! "And I don't want you talking to Mr. Drake, either," she grumbled, still uneasy about her decision the previous day to give Steven a chance. If she was wrong about him she didn't want Jennifer and Kelly getting hurt. They were already starting to idolize him.

"Aunt Lara!" Jennifer was clearly exasperated, her lower lip sticking out in a pout. Kelly was clinging to her sister's hand, her own face scrunching up in readiness for the first sign that a good noisy response was called for.

"You heard me. There are plenty of places to play on this farm without wandering off to that stream."

But the stream was the best place. Even she had to admit that. Pink stained her cheeks as she recalled the nights she'd spent there in Steven's arms. He'd brought the memory of those nights crashing back into her consciousness yesterday with that bold, yet tender kiss.

There had been that last glorious night when passion had soared without restraint, undimmed for her by the knowledge that these would be their final hours together. But what she remembered most was the first time they'd lain together on the banks of the stream.

A smile played about her lips at the memory. It had been the Fourth of July. She had been working in the fields, and she was hot and tired and sticky, streaks of dirt covering her from head to toe. Expecting to meet Steven at the barbecue in town, she had come to the stream for a quick swim and found him there waiting for her. A blanket had been spread on the grass, champagne was chilling in a bucket, and a bouquet of wildflowers had been tucked into a crystal vase.

"Is all this for me?" she'd asked, staring into his eyes in amazement.

"Who else would it be for?" he'd teased.

"But we were supposed to meet in town. How did you know I'd come?"

"You think you're so daring and unconventional, but in some ways, you're very predictable. On the days you've been working in the fields, you always come here for a swim before going to the house."

She'd wrinkled her nose at him. "I can see I'm going to have to start varying my patterns, or you'll grow entirely too sure of yourself."

"Never with you," he'd said, a smoldering heat replacing the tenderness and laughter in his eyes. "Never."

Lara had suddenly been struck by uncertainty. She had had a feeling right then that this would be a night like no other. Steven had held out his hand and led her, fully clothed, into the stream. Then, when the cool water swirled around them, he had washed the dirt from her face, brushed the wet tendrils of hair back from her cheeks and gently kissed her. Her arms had slid around his shoulders, her legs winding around his for balance. She had felt his body harden at once and, inexperienced as she was, had known a woman's satisfaction. There was an odd sense that the rebel had been tamed by her touch, that he was hers. Uncertainty had fled.

"Don't, Lara," he'd pleaded in a thick voice. "I want you so damn much, I won't be able to stop."

Her gaze steady, she'd said with disconcerting candor, "I don't want you to."

Steven had made a token protest. "Sweetheart, your parents and everyone will be expecting us in town. I didn't plan all this to seduce you."

She'd grinned at him. "Then I'll just have to seduce you, won't I?"

And she had, experimenting with touches, exploring with kisses, until his skin was on fire beneath her lips. Her cheeks burned as she recalled her reckless, wanton behavior.

With a final groan of submission he had carried her to the shore, placed her gently on the blanket and peeled away the wet clothes. Then he had made love to her, taking her again and again as dusk fell and shrouded them in the privacy of shadows. She had been a thirst he couldn't seem to quench. He had been a love whose nuances she never tired of discovering. Lying on their backs they'd been able to see the bright twinkle of the distant fireworks. It had been a moment of incredible beauty and perfection. Her heart had seemed filled to overflowing with sheer happiness.

Propped on an elbow he had gazed down at her, his expression gentle. "Are you sorry you missed the celebration?"

"Don't you know," she had said, her fingers against his lips, "the celebration was here."

It had been a timeless night, so filled with joy and laughter and excitement that she'd been certain it could never be matched. Only as the months wore on had she realized that each time in Steven's embrace was destined to be better than the last, shaded by the discovery of new emotions and the deepening of old ones.

Lara sighed at last as the vivid images began to fade. She glanced up and saw that Jennifer and Kelly had noticed her daydreaming and used her distraction to slip out of sight. She had no doubt at all they were headed straight for the stream. Jennifer had inherited the Danvers' stubbornness in full measure. Lara figured it would probably be to her benefit in the long run, but there were times like now when the child's single-mindedness thoroughly exasperated her.

"Jennifer, Kelly, I'm warning you," she shouted, starting after them. "Get back here right this minute, or you'll spend the rest of the day in your room."

Just then Jennifer burst through the stand of trees at the top of the knoll. Her clothes were smudged with dirt, and there were tears trickling down her cheeks. Even from this distance, Lara could see that her eyes were wide with fright. Her own heart rose to her throat.

"Aunt Lara, Aunt Lara, come quick!"

Her gaze scanned the edge of the woods, but she saw no sign of Kelly. "Jennifer, where's your sister? What's wrong?"

"S-s-something happened to K-K-Kelly." The words came out in a pitiful, scared tone.

Oh, dear God! The stream. It wasn't deep, but if Kelly had fallen and hurt her head, she could easily drown. Lara's heart slammed against her ribs. She set off at a run. "What happened? Did she fall in the water?"

"No-o-o."

Jennifer sobbed harder. Lara knelt in front of her and gathered the terrified child in her arms. "Honey, tell me, please. What happened?"

"S-s-she fell down, and I c-c-can't find her."

Lara choked back her own mounting hysteria. "What do you mean you can't find her? Is she hiding? Maybe she's just playing a game with you."

Jennifer shook her head. "She went in the ground, in a hole."

A terrible dawning apprehension swept through Lara, sending her pulse racing and a cold shiver of dread down her spine. "Oh, dear God." Spoken aloud this time, the words came out as a soft moan. "Show me where, Jennifer."

She picked Jennifer up in her arms and ran, stumbling, her arms aching under the child's weight. Despite her terror, she forced herself to speak calmly.

"Where were you? Show me exactly where you were the last time you saw her."

"Over there, Aunt Lara. We were right over there. I only let go of her hand for a minute. I swear it."

"Shh, baby. It's okay." She buried her face in Jennifer's hair and tried to soothe her. "Shh. We're going to get her."

But when they reached the old well, there was no sign of Kelly. They could hear only faint cries from a long way down. For a moment control fled and Lara panicked. Images of Kelly trapped in darkness, far from her reach made her sick.

Dear heaven, Lara prayed. Kelly can't die, not this way. Please, God, keep her safe.

The prayers steadied her. She peered down into the darkness and saw nothing.

"Kelly, sweetheart, Aunt Lara's here. Don't worry, baby, we'll get you out."

She studied the opening in the ground and wondered if she might not fit, then dismissed an inexpert rescue attempt as foolish. She had no way of knowing how far down Kelly was. She might even endanger her more by doing the wrong thing, and if she became trapped, as well, it certainly wouldn't do Kelly any good. There was no time for hesitation. She had to have help, and the nearest help was Steven. She would have to put her trust in him.

Taking a deep breath, she took hold of Jennifer's arms and said softly, "I want you to run to Mr. Drake's house as fast as you can. Can you do that for me? Tell him what's happened, and ask him to come quickly. I'll stay here with Kelly."

Tears streamed from Jennifer's frightened eyes. "I want to stay with you. I'm so-o-o s-s-scared, Aunt Lara."

"I'm scared, too, but it's going to be okay," she said with quiet conviction. She smoothed Jennifer's hair back from her face. "Listen. You can hear Kelly down there. She's just fine. You get Mr. Drake. He'll know what to do to get her out."

As soon as Jennifer had gone, Lara lay facedown flat on the ground and called down to Kelly, talking to her, crooning songs, listening for any sound that would tell her that her baby was okay.

She was like that when Steven arrived. She took one look at him, and the tears she'd been holding back began to fall. She flew into his arms seeking the comfort she knew she would find there. Pressed tightly against the warmth of his chest, she felt his strength seep into her. For the first time since he'd come charging back into her life, she was desperately grateful to see him.

The sight of Lara lying in the mud singing halting lullabies almost tore Steven's heart in two.

When Jennifer had arrived on his doorstep with tears streaming down her face, he'd had trouble understanding her garbled story. It was only when he found Lara that he realized in full what had happened. The poor woman must be scared out of her wits, though even through her tears the look she cast at him was every bit as strong and defiant as the look she'd worn when he'd first stumbled across them at the stream. There had been plenty of times when that streak of defiance had incensed him, but today he was grateful for it.

When she moved into his embrace, he felt her trembling for the first time in years. He realized then with absolute certainty that the hardness she'd been feigning covered deep emotions. Despite anger, despite denials, she still loved him. Thank God!

He knew what it had probably cost her not only to admit her need, but to turn to him. Her vulnerability made his heart leap, and a surge of fierce protectiveness washed through him. He had to bring Kelly safely back to her. He couldn't let her down, not if they were ever to have the future he wanted.

But as much as he wanted to hold her and comfort her, he knew if he was to succeed, there was no time to waste.

"How's she doing?" he asked in a level, quiet voice, wiping away the tears on her cheeks.

"She's crying." Lara's voice was filled with dismay.

"That's a good sign," he reassured her. "It tells us she's still okay. I left Jennifer with my housekeeper, and I've called for some help. As soon as they get here, we'll see what we can do about getting her out."

"Can't you just drop down a rope of something?"

"I think she's probably too young to know what to do. It might only make things worse. We're better off if she stays fairly still until we know what kind of ground we have down there."

"Dammit, I was counting on you. Why can't you do something now? We can't just leave her down there all alone." He saw the frustration written on her face, heard the rage of helplessness in her raised voice.

He led her away from the well. "There's no point in letting Kelly hear you. You'll frighten her."

Lara swallowed hard. He cupped her chin in his hand and forced her to meet his gaze. "Sweetheart, I know how you feel. Believe me, I do. Nothing is worse than waiting. I promise you as soon as we get some equipment, we'll go in after her. But if we don't do this right, the ground could cave in."

A visible shudder rippled through Lara at the horrible possibility he'd evoked, and instinctively Steven ran his hand down her back in a soothing gesture. "Don't worry, Lara. That's not going to happen. We'll get her out. I promise."

"I have to call Tommy. He has to know." She looked terrified by the prospect of making that call, her eyes huge and luminous in her pale face.

"Don't you want to wait a few minutes and see if we can't get her out right away?" Steven suggested.

"Do you think it will happen quickly?"

"No promises, but I hope so."

But it didn't.

The afternoon turned into an eternity. Logan was the first to arrive, giving her hand a sympathetic squeeze before turning to Steven for instructions. When the men from town arrived, they conferred with Steven, all but shutting Lara out of the discussion. To her fury she was drawn away from the edge of the well by the volunteer fire chief's wife. A cup of coffee was placed in her hands.

"Drink this," Terry Simmons said in her naturally gruff voice, her manner brisk but somehow comforting. "You're freezing. We can't have you going into shock on us. Kelly needs you."

Lara's gaze flew to the well, then sought out Steven. He gave her a reassuring smile that steadied her for the moment, then turned back to the discussion. A measuring device was lowered carefully into the well, and the conversation became more heated. From the occasional bits she could hear, Lara guessed they were arguing about the next step. Steven apparently prevailed, because he nodded in satisfaction, and the men began working.

It seemed to take forever before he finally left them and came to her. She searched his face for some sign of hope, but his expression was grim.

"It's not going the way you hoped, is it?"

"I'm afraid not. She's down a lot farther than I'd hoped. The well's not wide enough for any of us to go down after her."

"I could try," she said, frantic to do something. She kept envisioning Kelly growing more and more frightened the longer she was left all alone in the darkness. "I checked it earlier while I was waiting for you. I'm sure I'd fit."

He shook his head. "No. You wouldn't make it, either."

"How do you know? Steven, we have to do something, anything. Let me try."

"Dammit, you'd just tear your skin to shreds. Even if you made it into the well, it narrows considerably about ten feet down. You'd never get past that. I promise you I know what I'm doing. I've called for some drilling equipment."

"Why?" she asked, then recalled the rescue of the little Texas child that had drawn international attention. "You're going to create a tunnel alongside her, aren't you?"

"We're going to try that. With any luck, it should be a simple process."

But Lara remembered that the anguished plight of that family in Texas had gone on for more than two days. She closed her eyes, then faced him with a quiet question. "It's time I called Tommy now, isn't it?"

Steven took her hand and squeezed hard, refusing to lie to her. "I think so."

Hating the words, but grateful for his honesty, she tried for a brave smile. It faltered and tears formed in her eyes. "Dear God, I don't think I can stand this."

Steven's hands rested on her shoulders, and he looked evenly into her eyes. "You can. You're the strongest woman I know. Now I want you to come with me and reassure Kelly about what we're going to do. Then go call your brother."

At the edge of the well, the men parted for her. Logan was on the ground, playing a lively song on a hand-carved whistle just like the one he'd given Lara for Jennifer. When he stopped at the sight of Lara, she heard Kelly call out for more.

"I'll play you another one later, half pint. Your Aunt Lara's here now."

Lara dropped to her knees, then glanced up at Steven. He rested his hand on her shoulder. She took a deep, shuddering breath, then called down, "Kelly, can you hear me?"

"Aunt Lara?" The wavering words seemed to travel a great distance.

"Yes, honey, it's me."

"I hear you, Aunt Lara, but I can't see you." The sentence ended on a plaintive wail.

"I know you can't, baby, but I'm right here, just the same. Mr. Drake is with me, too. He's working to get you out of there."

"I want out now!"

Lara found herself grinning at the adamant tone. "It won't be too much longer."

"Warn her not to move around much," Steven whispered. "I don't want her slipping any deeper."

"Sweetheart, can you do something for me? Can you stay real still? There's going to be some loud noise in a little while, but I don't want you to be scared. It's just going to be some big machines trying to help you.''

''Will you stay with me?''

Lara glanced at Steven, but he shook his head. ''I'll have to move out of the way for a little while, but Mr. Drake will be real close, and he'll check on you, okay?''

''Want you,'' she said, her voice quivering.

''I won't be far away, baby, and pretty soon you'll be back up here with me.''

''Promise?''

''Cross my heart.'' Steven touched her arm, and she looked up to see that the drilling equipment had arrived and was in place. ''Kelly, I have to move now. You be really brave now, okay?''

''Okay. Bye, Aunt Lara.''

When Lara heard the spirited response, it raised a lump in her throat. She turned and found herself held in the ample arms of Terry Simmons.

''Come on, gal. You're doing just fine. Steven will take care of things from here on out.''

''I need to call Tommy.''

''Well, then, let's go do it.''

Forced to shoulder responsibility at an early age, Lara had never known what it was to rely on the strength of others. But even though she'd never exchanged more than a dozen sentences with her in the past, she found herself leaning on Terry Simmons. In her quiet, brusque way Terry kept her sane, kept her focused on what had to be done rather than what might happen. She was desperately appreciative of the older woman's company as she placed the call to Kansas City and told Tommy, in a voice that shook but didn't break, exactly what was happening with Kelly.

Tommy quickly grasped the seriousness of the situation. Thankfully he didn't waste time with accusations or hysterics. "I'll get Megan, and we'll be on the first plane."

Lara wanted to hold out some measure of hope. "She could be out before you get here."

"All the better. Let me go now, so I can make the arrangements."

"Tommy."

"Yes?"

"I'm so sorry." This time her voice did break; and she choked back a sob.

"Don't start crying, Sis," he begged, his own voice suddenly thick with unshed tears. "You've got to be strong until we get there. Tell our baby we love her."

"I'll tell her," she promised with forced bravery. "I'll see you soon."

Once she was off the phone, she and Terry went back to the well. Watching the rescue attempt, the brisk orders Steven gave and the quick response from the volunteers, she tried to relax, to concentrate on thinking positively, but her thoughts were in turmoil. She was racked by a terrible sense of guilt.

If only she'd been paying better attention, she told herself, this would never have happened. She'd become too complacent, thinking of the farm as a safe haven for herself and her nieces. She'd forgotten all about the old wells scattered around the property. Most had been topped off for years, but as kids she and her brothers had been attracted to them. Only dire threats of punishment had kept them from trying to pry loose the tops themselves. Obviously some other children had found them an irresistible challenge, unaware that they were leaving a deadly temptation behind.

"Lara." Steven's voice lured her back to the present. It was nearly dark now, the air cooling rapidly. Huge spotlights had been focused on the well.

"We've dug a shaft alongside her," he explained. "I'm going to try going down to see how close we are and see what we'll have to do to tunnel across."

"Why you?" she demanded unreasonably, needing a target for her frustration and falling instinctively back on the anger she'd felt toward him for so long. Terry Simmons stared at her in surprise. A brief shaft of hurt flickered in Steven's eyes, and she realized at once how horribly ungrateful she sounded. She sighed as she tried to grapple with tangled emotions. "I'm sorry. Thank you."

Their eyes clashed. She expected irritation in the wake of that instant of pain, but she found instead understanding.

"It's okay," he said. "I'm going because I know what I'm doing. The others don't."

With bated breath she watched as the men began to lower Steven into the newly dug shaft, watched as he disappeared from view, linked to the surface only by ropes and frantic hands.

Then she watched in growing dismay as the faces of the men fell. Logan shook his head and turned away. Her heart sank to its lowest point yet as Steven re-emerged alone.

Five

—

Lara watched Steven's approach with a growing sense of alarm. His expression was discouraged, the lines in his face etched deeper. As he came closer, he smiled, but there was so much bone weariness in the effort she wasn't reassured at all.

"Is she d-d...?" She couldn't get the word past trembling lips.

Steven's arms came around her at once. "No. Oh, sweetheart, no. She's not dead. She was chattering to me the whole time I was down there." His fingers brushed her cheek, and this time when he smiled, it reached his eyes. "Your niece has quite a temper. She's mad as blazes because she thinks Jennifer will get her share of the homemade ice cream you told them you'd make tonight. I swore to her that she could have all the ice cream she wanted when she got out."

Relieved, but still not convinced that he was telling her the entire truth, she said, "But you looked so sad."

"We ran up against a problem I hadn't anticipated, that's all. It's just going to take us a little longer to get to her than I would have liked."

"Why?"

"The ground is rockier down there. It'll take us a while to cut our way through. I want to go slowly, so we don't make any mistakes." He brushed the hair from her face and studied her closely. The gentle caress renewed her strength.

"Are you going to be okay?" he asked.

"I'll be fine. Just get her out safely."

Hour after hour the tension grew. The night dragged on interminably. Kelly's cheerful chatter diminished to tired whimpers and then nothing at all. Though Steven refused to even acknowledge the possibility, Lara feared they had lost her.

"Lara, come with me and get something to eat," Terry insisted.

"I can't leave," she protested wearily, though she knew if she didn't rest soon she would collapse from fatigue. The strain was telling on her. Her body ached all over from the constant tension in her muscles. Her head throbbed. There was a gnawing sensation in the pit of her stomach that went beyond hunger.

"You don't have to leave. The ladies from town have set up a food tent for the men. You can eat right here."

Lara glanced around in amazement at the make-shift kitchen that had sprung up less than fifty yards away without her even noticing. Tables and folding chairs were scattered around an area lit by lanterns. Behind a buffet table several women she recognized were serving slices of ham, scoops of potato salad and coleslaw to the workers.

Sighing, she gave in to Terry's urgings. She went over to the women, grateful beyond words for their support.

"Thank you," she began, and then couldn't go on.

Terry interceded. "Go on and sit down. I'll bring the food right over."

Lara found an empty chair from which she could still see the rescue operation and sank down on it. Her eyes burned from the strain of watching and waiting and from holding back scalding tears.

"Here you go," Terry said, putting a plate down in front of her.

Lara stared at the food with disinterest.

"Eat. You ain't gonna do that child a bit of good if you go falling apart."

"It's my fault she's down there," Lara blurted out, almost relieved to say the words aloud. "I should have watched her more closely."

"Honey, there's not a parent alive who doesn't think that when his child gets hurt. You go right on thinking it, even when they're grown. The truth of the matter is you can't keep watch over 'em every second of the day. There's always gonna be a time when you turn your back for just a minute. Any kid with the least bit of mischief in him is gonna use that time to slip away."

"I feel so awful, though. Tommy and Megan trusted me. I encouraged them to leave the kids with me for the summer. I wasn't ready to part with them yet. Kelly's like my own daughter. Jennifer's just like Tommy, but Kelly reminds me of the way I used to be. Even as a baby she had so much spirit."

"Don't you think that spirit will help her get through this?"

"But she's still so little."

"All the more reason for hope. She's probably too young to know exactly how much danger she's in. She'll be taking her cues from you and Steven and the other men. If you can manage to put aside your own fears and treat this like an adventure, she'll hang in there."

"God, I hope so." Lara tried a bite of the ham under Terry's watchful gaze, then the potato salad. It could have been boiled leather for all the attention she gave it. She glanced over at the women who were putting out more food.

"Why did they come?" she asked, genuinely bewildered by their generosity. "I don't even know most of them. I mean I know their names, but I've never really gotten to know them."

"Even though Toledo's sprawling closer all the time, this is still country. Times like this, neighbors rally around. We'd have been here for you when your mama died, too, but you made it pretty plain you wanted to be left on your own."

Lara shook her head ruefully, recalling how her pride had kept her from accepting even a kind word back then. She could remember practically slamming the door in the faces of some of the people who had come to call. Torn apart by grief and fear of the responsibilities ahead, she had irrationally blamed everyone for her mother's death, blamed them for not helping her to shoulder the impossible burden of running a farm. If they'd helped, she'd been so sure her mother would have lived.

"I was so angry back then," she admitted.

"You had a right to be. First losing your daddy and then your mama. We all knew how much you gave up when you came home from school to take care of your brothers. That's a heavy load for a young girl. We all admired how you pitched right in and took over here. You kept this place going as well as your daddy could have. Better, some say."

"But I was rude and selfish in refusing your offers of help."

"That's in the past."

"Maybe so, but I've been thinking about the past a lot lately. I made my share of mistakes, too. I was just so afraid of relying on anyone back then. It wasn't just my parents dying, but . . ." Her voice trailed off when she realized what she'd been about to confess.

"Steven?" Terry prompted. At Lara's look of astonishment, the older woman smiled. "We all knew you'd fallen for him like a ton of bricks. A blind man could've seen that. Those blue eyes of yours sure did shine the minute they set on him. As for Steven, he looked like he wasn't quite sure what hit him. A man like that, a man who's been on his own, traveling around, he's not the type to give up his freedom easily, but everybody in town was taking bets on when you'd get him to the altar."

"It didn't work out."

"We all wondered about it when he left so suddenly. You poked that chin of yours up in the air and looked so proud, we were all sure you'd given him the boot, but that wasn't the way it was, was it?"

Lara sighed and shook her head. "He left me."

"And now? From the way that man looks at you, my guess is he's still in love with you. Has been ever since he came back to town, assuming he ever stopped."

"So he says."

"But you still don't trust him?"

"How can I?" Lara's voice was wistful.

"Give it time, girl. Trust isn't something you have to give or withhold overnight. It's earned." Lara glanced toward the well where Steven's yellow hard hat was visible in the midst of the throng of men. "Seems to me he's trying mighty hard to prove something to you. Listen with your head, but don't ignore your heart."

Lara instinctively reached across the table and clasped the other woman's hand. She somehow felt closer to Terry Simmons than she had to any woman since her mother died. It was as though in the midst of this tragedy, she had found a friend. "Thank you. I hope we won't go back to being strangers when this is over."

"Child, I'm always around. That husband of mine thinks a trip to the grocery is enough traveling. You just call whenever you need me."

Just then Lara heard her name shouted by a familiar voice.

Leaping to her feet, she looked around until she saw Tommy and Megan coming toward her. Afraid to anticipate their reaction to her, she took a hesitant step forward then waited. Then Tommy opened his arms, and she ran into them. Only the desperate tightness of his embrace indicated the depth of his distress.

"How is she, Sis?"

"Steven says she's doing okay. He refuses to give up hope."

Tommy's eyebrows rose fractionally. "Steven?"

"I had to send for him," Lara said defensively. "He knows about this sort of thing."

Megan shot an irritated look at her husband. "Of course, you should have called on him. Can we talk to him? I want to hear what's happening with my baby."

Lara nodded. "I'll take you to him." She grasped Megan's hand, and with Tommy on the other side of her, they crossed the stretch of land to the rescue site. Steven broke away from the cluster of men as soon as he saw them. He held out his hand and after an instant's hesitation, Tommy shook it.

"What have you done so far?" Tommy asked.

Quickly and unemotionally, Steven brought them up-to-date on the efforts to free Kelly. "I've got someone down there now bringing out rocks. It's tedious work, and all we can do in the meantime is wait."

"Surely there must be something more," Tommy said. "Don't worry about the expense. We'll find the money somehow."

"It's not a question of money. Hell, if it were, I'd gladly pay it myself. This is just something that takes time. The last thing we want to do is rush the job and cause a cave-in."

Megan gasped at his words. Steven instantly reached out to squeeze her hand. "Don't worry. It's not going to happen."

"Can I talk to her?"

Steven and Lara exchanged glances. It was Lara who responded. "She's been asleep for a while now. I think all of this wore her out."

Megan's eyes widened, and for the first time the realization of her daughter's danger hit her fully. She bit her lip and gazed helplessly up at Tommy, then back at Lara. "Are you sure...are you really sure she's asleep?"

Lara swallowed her own doubts and embraced her sister-in-law. "I believe that with all my heart."

"What about Jennifer?" Tommy asked. "Who's taking care of her?"

"She's at my house," Steven said. "Mrs. Marston, my housekeeper, is with her. You're welcome to go over there and spend some time with her. It'll be a while before anything happens here."

Megan nodded. "I need to see her."

Tommy looked so torn that Lara finally stepped in. She could readily understand Megan's need to see for herself that her other child was all right. "I'll take her," she told Tommy. "You stay here and do what you can to help."

He looked at her gratefully. "Thanks, Sis. Tell Jennifer I love her."

Outside Steven's house, Lara found herself slowing her steps. Megan regarded her curiously. "Are you okay?"

"I just never thought I'd be setting foot inside this house."

Even though it was well past midnight, Mrs. Marston had apparently been awake. She threw open the front door just then. "Is there any word on the little one yet?"

"Not yet, I'm afraid. I'm Lara Danvers."

"I recognize you, girl," she said readily, and Lara assumed it was because she'd seen her around town. It wasn't until they were upstairs that she realized it was more than that. As Megan went in to sit beside her sleeping daughter, Lara couldn't resist peeking into the master bedroom to see if it had been built the way she and Steven had planned it all those years ago. What she found took her breath away.

The bay window had exactly the view they'd envisioned, the window seat deep and padded with comfortable cushions. The bed was large enough to readily accommodate two tall people with a penchant for tossing in their sleep. It was what she found on the stand beside the bed that really threw her, though. In a small silver frame there was a copy of the one picture ever taken of her and Steven together. No wonder the housekeeper had recognized her. It must have puzzled her all these years to see a picture of a woman who lived so near yet never appeared in person.

Lara picked up the picture and carried it with her as she walked around the room. She remembered the morning it had been taken. It had been a few days after Christmas. Sun had sparkled on the icicles dangling from the barn roof and on the fine layer of snow that had dusted the ground. She and Steven had been riding hard, their breath visible in the cold air. When they galloped back to the barn, they found Tommy there playing with the inexpensive camera that had been his Christmas present. He'd insisted on taking a picture of the two of them. Lara's hair was in golden disarray, her cheeks colored pink by the wintry chill in the air. Steven had looked bigger and bolder than ever in his jeans and sheepskin jacket. The expression in his eyes had been that of a lover. Tommy, for all his lack of skill with a camera, had managed to capture the secret smile that passed between them. It was a stirringly sensual picture.

She carried it with her as she wandered into the master bathroom. Turning her gaze from the picture she discovered a huge tub and, to her absolute delight, a skylight.

"So we could always see the fireworks," Steven murmured startling her.

Lara whirled around. He was standing in the doorway watching her, an unreadable expression on his face.

"You remembered," she said softly.

"Sentimental, huh?"

"It's something I would never have guessed about you, but I like it."

"You found the picture, too?"

She held it out guiltily. "Sorry. I'm afraid I was snooping."

"It doesn't matter. Do you like the house?"

"I love it."

"I built it for you." When she would have spoken, he held up his hand. "I know. I wasn't sure you'd ever set foot inside the place, but I wanted to be prepared. I couldn't do any less than what we'd talked about."

"And the picture?"

"It made me feel closer to you. Do you still have yours?"

She nodded. "It's in a drawer. I couldn't throw it away."

"Lara . . ." He broke off, looking confused.

"What is it? Has something happened to Kelly?"

"No. In fact, I think we may be getting very close to reaching her. I thought you and Megan would want to know."

Her eyes lit up. "I'll get Megan right away."

"There's just one thing I'd like to do first." He stepped toward her, and Lara's heart began a wild drumming. He tilted her chin up and searched her eyes for the longest time until she was sure the kiss would never happen. When his lips settled across hers at first, they were gentle and slightly tentative. But as she opened her mouth to him, he became bolder, hungrily taking what she offered. It was a lingering, breath-stealing kiss, yet somehow edged with caution. It was as though Steven feared demanding too much, feared that her acceptance might just as easily turn to rejection.

But Lara couldn't have turned him away if she'd wanted to. He was fulfilling dreams she'd had on too many nights. She was mystified by this power he had over her, awed by it. In many ways she feared it, as she'd feared little else in recent years.

His lips moved lightly on hers, the deep, drugging kiss followed now by quick, affectionate ones. At last he sighed heavily and reluctantly drew away.

"You can't imagine how many times I've imagined you here with me, in my arms. Now that you're really here, it's all I can do to let you go."

"We have to tell Megan the news. We have to go back."

"Of course we do." His eyes blazed with promise. "But when this is over, Lara, you won't get away so easily."

When they reached the well, he settled her and Megan just beyond the work area and went to check on the progress that had been made. While he was gone, Lara found herself scanning the crowd to find him, taking her strength from his quiet self-confidence, finding it in a glance that told her again and again he understood her pain, her fears, her desperation for some new ray of hope.

Watching him work companionably with the men from town, she realized with a start that he was no longer an outsider. At some point since his return, the bold hit-and-run developer of eleven years ago had become an accepted, even respected member of the community.

At last he came over to the two of them and held out his hand. A smile played about his lips.

"Come with me."

A part of her wanted to resist, to stay back here on the fringes where she could keep desolation at bay, but Megan was already starting forward, excitement in her eyes. Lara hung back for an instant.

"Why?" she asked, afraid to get her hopes up despite the look on his face.

"Just come."

She put her hand in his and felt his warmth steal through her. Slowly he led her back to the well.

"Listen," he said softly.

Lara strained to hear, and when she did, tears welled up and spilled down her cheeks. Megan's cheeks were similarly damp. The sound was weak and came from very far away. The words were halting, but Lara had no doubt about what she heard. Kelly was singing the words to the song Logan had taught her earlier.

Lara lifted shining eyes to Steven.

"Thank you."

Megan nodded. "You have no idea how badly I needed to hear that."

"I think maybe I do," he said, and gently brushed away Lara's tears as Tommy came to hold Megan. Lara clung to Steven, her head resting against his chest where she could hear the steady beat of his heart. "Lara, I can't tell you not to be scared. You have every right to be terrified. Just know that I want that little girl out of there safely every bit as badly as you do. Even though you and I have had our problems, there's nothing in this world I wouldn't do to try to save that child."

Lara swallowed. "I know you're trying. If...if it doesn't work out, I won't blame you."

Steven touched a rough finger to her lips. "Only positive thoughts are allowed around here, okay?"

"Okay." She met his gaze and found something unexpected there, an intensity that under other circumstances would have made her blood race. Unable to cope with it, she glanced away.

"It won't be long now," he promised.

Still, the tedious process seemed to drag on interminably through the morning and afternoon. Steven was there for her. When her words faltered, he seemed to know what it was she'd meant to say. He continued to give her uncommon strength with a single glance, a whispered encouragement.

When the sun began to set on the second day of the ordeal, Lara sat shivering in the cool evening air. Megan was with Tommy, and she was once again alone with only her thoughts for company. Terry lingered nearby, but as if she understood Lara's unspoken need for solitude, she waited for some sign that she was needed again.

Floodlights lit the scene, giving it an eerie sense of unreality. The sound of drilling had ceased, and only the low murmur of conversation and hushed directions penetrated the silence.

When Steven approached, his handsome face streaked with dirt, Lara felt the knot of tension in her stomach ease. He dropped down beside her. She reached out tentatively and brushed a streak of dirt from his cheek.

"I think we're finally ready to do it," he said, capturing her hand and holding it tightly.

Lara swallowed. They were the words she'd been waiting forever to hear, but now they frightened her. What if this rescue failed? Worse, what if they reached Kelly, and it was too late?

"I think you should stay back here, though. This could take a while." She knew from what he left unsaid that he shared her fears and wanted to spare her if they had failed.

"Are you going down?"

"Yes."

She rubbed a finger gently across the scrapes and bruises on his knuckles. "Then you'll get her out."

"Lara . . ."

"No, don't. I have to believe that. I have to believe in you."

"Lara, I could fail."

She put her hands over her ears and pretended not to have heard, though the bleak words echoed through her head.

"You will bring her back to me." She glanced at Megan and Tommy, whose eyes were filled with heartache as they waited. "You'll bring her back to us."

She had no idea of the exact moment when bitterness and hatred had turned to trust again, but it had, and it was the only thing that warmed her now.

She followed Steven with her eyes as he returned to the site, watched as he donned his hard hat and draped cables and tools around his waist. Just before he stepped to the opening, his gaze swept the perimeter of the crowd and found her. He gave her a jaunty thumbs-up gesture, which she returned with a trembling hand.

Despite Steven's warning that she should stay back, she was drawn closer and closer to the raw opening that had been cut in the earth. An ambulance and a team of paramedics stood by.

"What's taking so long?" Lara murmured, tension twisting inside her. She imagined all the terrible things that could go wrong. She folded her arms across her middle and held on for dear life. Nervously her fingers bit into the soft flesh of her upper arms as the wait dragged on.

A quiet stirring of excitement drew her attention. She saw the fire chief smile, then heard an eruption of sound at his announcement. "He's got her. He's bringing her out."

Six

As the word spread, a cheer arose. Lara crept closer, holding her breath now, peering into the pool of light that centered on that gaping hole. She saw the flash of his bright yellow hat as Steven began to emerge.

And then she could see Kelly, blinking at the bright lights, rubbing grubby hands across her dirt-streaked cheeks. She cuddled closer to Steven's chest and buried her face in his shoulder, then peeked out beguilingly. When her smile came at last, Lara released her breath and ran to her.

Megan and Tommy were there before her. Casting a regretful glance in Lara's direction, Steven placed Kelly carefully into Megan's waiting arms. Despite the rightness of his action, Lara felt suddenly lost and alone until Steven reached for her hand and held it tightly, his gaze filled with compassion and under-

standing. Megan was openly weeping, her brave fa-
cade gone now that she actually had her baby back.
Even the normally stoic Tommy had a suspicious
glimmer of dampness at the corners of his eyes.

"Mommy! Daddy!" Kelly exclaimed in a tired but
excited voice. "You came to see me."

When Megan and Tommy couldn't seem to get a
word out, Lara said, "Of course, they did, baby. You
gave your mommy and daddy and me quite a scare."

"I not like it down there."

Steven spoke up then. "I think it might be a good
idea if you took her to the hospital to get checked out.
She seems just fine, but it's best to be sure."

Tommy nodded. "We'll take her right away."

He paused, as if something else were on his mind.
Lara knew he was struggling with mixed emotions
about owing such a debt to a man he'd come to hate
on her behalf. Though she knew in the end he would
say the right thing, she decided to make it easier for
him.

"Steven, I don't know if we'll ever be able to thank
you enough for what you did," she said, lifting her
gaze to meet his, sending him a message that went far
deeper than mere appreciation.

"No thanks are necessary."

"Yes, they are," Tommy said quietly. "You saved
our little girl. We owe you."

"Just make sure she grows up to be as lovely as her
Aunt Lara," Steven responded, his eyes never leaving
hers. "That'll be thanks enough."

Tommy apparently caught the heated look passing
between Lara and Steven, because he frowned. Me-

gan prevented him from saying anything by stepping in and reminding him that they needed to take Kelly to the hospital.

"We'll see you back at the house then," Tommy told Lara.

Steven met Lara's gaze, sending a clear, urgent request that made her tremble. "No," she said to Tommy. "You and Megan need to be alone with Kelly tonight. I'll stay at Steven's. We'll bring Jennifer back in the morning."

Tommy started to argue, but Megan again intervened. "Fine. We'll see you all in the morning. Come over in time for breakfast."

When they had gone, Steven cast her a rueful glance. "I don't think your brother approves."

"He's always been very protective of me. He'll come around."

Steven smiled. "I guess if I can win you over, Tommy should be a piece of cake."

"Does his approval matter to you?"

"Only because I know how very much it matters to you. Now let's see that everything here is wrapped up and be on our way."

For the first time Lara recalled all the people who had come to help and were now busy cleaning up. She circled through the crowd thanking each one of them. As they voiced their delight about the outcome of the rescue, she was once again moved by the genuine kindness and generosity of people she had deliberately turned from for so many years. When she came to Terry Simmons, she hugged her without restraint, still surprised by the depth of her feelings for this woman she'd barely known forty-eight hours earlier.

"I couldn't have gotten through the last two days without you," she admitted with uncommon candor.

"Posh-tosh, girl. You're a survivor. But if I was able to ease things a little for you, I'm glad. Just don't be a stranger now. My door's always open."

"Thank you."

When she was alone with Steven at last, he draped an arm around her shoulders. "Let's go home."

Home. The word sent a thrill through her. Oh, if it was only true. For the moment, though, she would take whatever comfort tonight offered and pray that tomorrow would take care of itself. The near tragedy had already reminded her of so many things she had nearly lost. She wouldn't give Steven up again, not if she could help it.

This time when she reached Steven's house with him by her side, it felt like a homecoming. He gazed down at her, his eyes darkening to the intense blue of a nighttime sea. "I feel as though I should be carrying you across the threshold, but I'm not sure I have the strength left."

She placed her hand against his cheek, then gently touched the lines of exhaustion on his brow. "We'll save that for another time. It's enough for me just to be coming here with you."

"I hope you didn't feel pressured into coming," he said, sounding suddenly contrite.

She grinned. "All you did was look at me," she retorted lightly. "I made the decision."

"Knowing that iron will of yours, I suppose I should never have doubted it." He held out a hand. "Come on, then. Let's go in."

The front door had barely closed behind them, when Mrs. Marston appeared, her face alight with a broad smile. "I heard on the news. The little one is okay."

"She seems to be fine," Lara said.

"I'm so glad." She peered anxiously at Steven. "And you're okay, too? No cuts and scrapes under all that dirt?"

He chuckled. "Don't worry. I'll clean up before I sit on the furniture."

Mrs. Marston grew flustered. "I was not suggesting for one moment..." she began, her cheeks turning bright pink.

Lara chuckled. "If you weren't, you should have been. He is a mess."

"Okay," he grumbled lightly. "I get the message. I'll go take a shower."

"Would you like dinner?"

"Perhaps just some sandwiches and a pot of chamomile tea. Is that okay with you, Lara?"

"Fine."

"You can leave them in the living room, Mrs. Marston. I'll be back down shortly."

As he left the room, Mrs. Marston turned to Lara. "If I might, could I suggest you go up to see your niece for a few minutes. She's been a little restless tonight. I think it would do her a world of good to know that her sister's okay."

"I'll go right up," Lara said, following Steven up the stairs.

He apparently heard her coming, because he waited for her at the top, then caught her in his arms. Anticipation sent her pulse racing.

"I can't wait another moment to do this," he said before lowering his lips to hers. Her soft curves fit snugly against the hard planes of his body, and heat flooded through her. Her arms slid around his shoulders, and she felt herself lifted up on tiptoe as he shifted her even more tightly against him. He smelled of dirt and sweat and warm masculinity, the strong odors oddly erotic to her senses. His touch was brashly possessive and confident now, stroking her skin in a way that left a wake of fire. His hands cupped her buttocks and urged her against the hard evidence of his arousal. As it had all those years ago, it created a warm feeling of purely feminine satisfaction. The magic had not left her touch.

Or his.

She was burning, her body awakening from its long slumber to a white-hot siege of desire. She was rapidly slipping beyond thought into a whirlwind of feelings. Forgotten were Steven's shower, the food being prepared downstairs, even the past, as she was swept away by the delight of the present.

And then she heard the soft whimper. It was little more than a sigh, but it did what nothing else could have done. It drew her back to reality.

"Jennifer," Steven said, sighing heavily.

She nodded. "I'm sorry."

"Don't be, love. It's probably just as well. I want to savor every minute of this, and I was in grave danger of losing control and taking you right here in the hall."

"An interesting thought," she commented, then gave him an impish smile. "Hold onto it."

He playfully slapped her backside as she twirled away from him. "I'll see you downstairs."

Steven found himself singing in the shower. Exhaustion vanished under the hard, steamy spray of water. He hadn't felt this alive in years. He knew Lara was responsible. Her absence had taught him that much. He could exist without her. He had become successful at business, sought after by women, highly regarded by his friends, but it had meant nothing. He had felt empty inside. Only Lara had been able to fill the emptiness, to make him whole. His sweet, sensuous, spirited Lara. This time he would never let her go.

Though he'd departed years ago with the very best intentions, he regretted leaving more than he could ever tell her. He felt responsible for the dimming of the bright light that had once shone in her eyes, for the sadness that had replaced it. If it was within his power, he would give her back the spirit and laughter he had taken from her. At the very least he would spend a lifetime trying.

Anxious to be with her, to explore the satin texture of her skin, to smell the fragrance of her body's natural perfume, to bury himself in her warmth, he hurried with his dressing. He ran his fingers through his damp hair, yanked on clean jeans, then pulled on a shirt that he didn't bother to button as he walked barefoot down the hall to the guest room where Jennifer had been staying.

The vision that greeted him was like something out of a dream. Jennifer was drawn up on her side under a sheet, her blond hair a halo of wispy curls against her flushed cheeks. Lara was sitting on the floor beside the bed, her head resting against the edge, her own blond hair spilling over her shoulders. The long waves gleamed in the faint glow of the bedside lamp. One hand, the nails broken, but looking delicate and lovely nonetheless, rested on Jennifer's shoulder in a tender caress.

As he drew closer, Steven realized Lara had fallen asleep. Her breath rose and fell lightly, her lips parted as though awaiting a kiss. Her position appeared thoroughly uncomfortable, and yet she looked utterly at peace. He found himself staring at her, his breath caught in his throat in wonder. How had he ever walked away from her? How had he left behind such an inviting woman who'd been filled with such tempestuous passion? It had been the act of a fool.

Yet if he'd stayed back then or taken her with him, he might very well have destroyed the way they felt for each other. He'd known nothing of love in his life. His parents' marriage had been a bitter mockery, and their hatred of each other had created indifference, sometimes even animosity toward him. His own brief marriage had been an immature attempt at rebellion. He had basked in the warm glow, not only of Lara's open display of emotion, but in the laughter and affection of her whole family. He had wanted so much to be a part of what they had, and yet he had feared that his own inadequacies were too great, that he would never learn to give as unselfishly as they did.

For a while after he'd left, he'd done his best to prove his decision right. He'd become colder, more driven than ever, his manner, to all but a few, harsh or indifferent. But each time he had pulled away or exploded in anger, guilt plagued him. He saw Lara's face, heard her chiding him. Then, her point made, she would open her arms to him just the same, loving him in spite of himself. Sooner or later, he had had to come back to a love like that.

His discovery that she had never wed had saddened him when he considered the waste. Yet he had been undeniably grateful. She had not moved beyond his reach after all. Few second chances were granted in life, and he intended to make the most of this one.

Now, though he could have gazed at her for hours, at last he whispered, "Lara."

Blue eyes blinked open in confusion. Then her lips curved into an enticing smile. "Hi," she murmured sleepily.

"Hi, yourself. Maybe I should get you into bed and forget about dinner."

"You keep having the most interesting ideas."

"That one's not interesting," he said with regret. "You're obviously exhausted."

"Oh, you meant to put me into bed alone."

"It might be wise. The past two days have been quite an ordeal."

"We were never wise, Steven. Please, don't let's start now."

He drew in a sharp breath at the blatant appeal in her voice. "What am I going to do with you, Lara Danvers?"

"Just love me."

"Oh, sweetheart, I do. I will."

He helped her to her feet, but when she would have come directly into his arms, he shook his head and steered her from the room. "Dinner first."

Before they'd reached the living room, where a huge tray of sandwiches had been left on a table beside the open window, Steven was convinced that he wasn't hungry. He had only urged the dinner to give Lara time to reconsider, to be sure she wasn't simply caught up in the drama of the past two days and being swept away on a tide of overwhelming emotions. But when he tasted the first bite of food, he realized how long it had been since he'd eaten. He'd finished three sandwiches before he even said another word to the woman who was watching him with amusement.

"I would have sworn a few minutes ago that this was a delaying tactic," she taunted.

"It was," he confessed. Then he grinned at her. "Now that I'm satisfied, though, I have another hunger nagging at me."

"And what's that?" The question was all innocent curiosity, but the gleam in her eyes was pure seduction.

"You, my sweet." He beckoned. "Come here."

Though her hands trembled, she rose and came to him, standing before him tall and proud. He reached out and clasped her hands to still them. "Please, don't be afraid of me."

"I'm not. I'm afraid of us," she admitted. "Of what you do to me."

Her candor surprised him, but he understood at once exactly what she meant. He, too, was awed by the power of the emotions that had captured them and held them both for so many years. "We can wait."

A faint smile tugged at her lips. "Maybe you can, but I've already been waiting for eleven years. Love me, Steven. Please."

A groan tore through him. His blood surged, hot and swift. He was on his feet at once, sweeping her into his arms and carrying her back up the stairs.

"I feel like the trembling maiden in some Gothic novel," she said, the words whispered against his bare chest, her arms slipping past his shirt to caress the taut muscles of his back. "As if I'm being carried off to meet my fate."

"I am your fate," he whispered. "I'll prove that to you tonight."

When they reached his room, Lara was anything but a shy, trembling maiden. Her touch was bold as she anxiously stripped away his shirt, then ran her hands lovingly over his chest and shoulders until he was weak with wanting her. When she touched the snap on his jeans, his control reached its limits. He brushed her hands aside and fumbled with the buttons of her blouse, not satisfied until it had been swept away and her breasts were spilling into his hands. She gave a low moan as he urged the rosy nipples into hard peaks. The contrast of textures, the soft silk of her breasts and the pebbled crown, sent a tremor of delight straight through him. When he bent his head to take each one in his mouth, she arched her back and uttered a little cry of pleasure that made the flame inside him burn brighter.

He slid her jeans and bikini briefs down her long legs, lingering to taste the creamy softness of her thighs, the delicate curve of her calf, the dainty arch of her foot. Her flesh was cool when he began, but with each touch it grew more heated, her cries more anxious.

He placed her gently on the bed at last, then stood gazing down at her, reveling in the sight of her flushed skin, the curling triangle of hair at the apex of her thighs, the proud tilt of her breasts. Her eyes were limpid pools of longing. When she held out her arms to him, his last shred of control vanished, and he stripped off his remaining clothes and stretched out beside her.

"You are so beautiful," he whispered as the pale light of moonbeams whispered across her body. "You're exactly the way I remembered you."

"You told me I'd gotten skinny."

"I must have been crazy. All the curves are still here, and I want to explore every one of them."

"Do you plan on one of the long Lewis and Clark expeditions?" she inquired in a tone that was equal parts of amusement and impatience.

He touched a finger to the pulse at the base of her throat, then drew a delicate path to the tip of her breast. Her eyes closed as a tiny gasp escaped before she could hold it back.

"I just want this to be good for you," he said, intensifying his touch. "I don't want to hurry you."

"Then I'm afraid you'll have to keep your hands to yourself."

He shook his head. "You're asking the impossible."

"In that case," she began, and before he realized her intention, she had lifted herself on top of him until she was astride his thighs, "I'd better take charge."

Laughing, he said, "There's never been a time since I've known you that you weren't in charge."

"Just one," she said, her eyes suddenly sad.

Steven would have given anything to take back the words. He wrapped his arms around her and drew her down to rest against his chest. "I'm sorry. I didn't mean to remind you of all that, especially not now."

His hands caressed her, running down the curve of her spine. She trembled beneath the touch, and he deepened the strokes, lingering where he seemed to be pleasuring her the most. He felt her hot tears fall on his shoulder, but when he would have stopped to comfort her, she pleaded with him to go on.

"Just love me, Steven. I need you. Please."

Unable to stem the flow of her tears or to deny her plea, he poised above her, then met the upward thrust of her hips with a long, deep stroke that plunged him into the center of her warmth. Though he'd intended to be slow and gentle, his control snapped at the exquisite rightness of the sensation. Captivated by her once more, his body rejoiced in the joining, leading her, then following, until they both exploded in a glorious fury of fire with the promise of eternity.

Seven

Fingers of sunlight crept into the room until they brushed across Lara's bare shoulders. She felt the gentle strokes of golden warmth and awoke with a sleepy, satisfied smile. Even without the bright promise of dawn, today would have been a day to celebrate. Not only was Kelly safe and well, but love, the most precious of all gifts, had been given back to her.

Still not quite able to believe it, she rolled to her side and touched Steven's cheek. Caressing the light stubble of his beard and the warmth of his skin reassured her that last night had not been a dream. He was very real, and as a lover he was everything she'd remembered—gentle and considerate, demanding, yet giving far more than he took. Though the emotional and physical cost of the rescue must have been high, Steven had not let her see it. He had shown her only the strength and tenderness and passion that had been missing from her life for so long. Through the night he had reawakened her senses, until her body sang once more with the joy of being desired and fulfilled.

"Only with you, dear one," she whispered, her touch lingering on his cheek. "Only with you."

Suddenly she heard a scampering in the hallway. The door to the room burst open.

"Aunt Lara! Aunt Lara!" Jennifer shouted excitedly, before skidding to a stop at the sight of Steven. She regarded him with a puzzled frown.

Thoroughly disconcerted by the intrusion, Lara dragged the sheet up to her neck. She glanced down to discover that Steven had opened one eye to see what all the fuss was about. Her obvious discomfort brought a grin to his lips, but he quickly banished it as he waited in infuriating silence to see how she planned to handle the awkward situation. She glared at him, wondering if there was any way the floor could open up and swallow the two of them. Or, perhaps, only Steven.

Before she could think of some explanation to offer her silent, wide-eyed niece, Mrs. Marston hurried into the room, her apron flapping, her lips pursed.

"So, there you are," she said to Jennifer. "I thought I told you that your aunt was still asleep and that you weren't to go bothering her."

"But I knew she wouldn't mind if I woke her up," Jennifer protested indignantly. "I had to look really hard to find her."

She peered at Steven again. "Why are you here, Mr. Drake?" she asked in a voice that was both confused and unconsciously prim.

Lara shot a fierce scowl of warning in his direction, and Steven promptly choked back a laugh.

"Well," he said, clearing his throat and carefully avoiding her eyes. Lara awaited his explanation with almost as much interest as Jennifer. "Umm. Actually your Aunt Lara had a bad dream during the night. I came in to make sure she was okay, and I guess I fell asleep."

It was a noble attempt and Lara loved him for it, but Jennifer still appeared skeptical. "But you don't have any clothes on," she pointed out.

This time it was Lara who had to swallow hard to keep from chuckling. There was no denying Steven's state of undress, not with nothing more than a discreetly placed sheet between him and total embarrassment. Fortunately Mrs. Marston, her own lips twitching with mirth, saved the day by taking Jennifer firmly by the hand.

"Come along, young lady, and let your aunt get dressed if you want to get home to see your sister."

Jennifer's eyes brightened. "Oh, yes, please hurry, Aunt Lara. I want to see Kelly and Mommy and Daddy."

"Okay, sweetheart. I'll be as fast as I can," Lara promised.

When the door had closed behind her niece, Lara hardly dared to meet Steven's gaze. When she did, his eyes glittered brightly and dangerously.

"I suppose you'll have to marry me now," he said lightly. Lara's eyes widened. "Otherwise it'll be Jennifer prodding us all the way to the church with a shotgun. Do you suppose she gets that stern, disapproving attitude from her father?"

"What I think is that we took her by surprise. I doubt if she fully understood the implications."

"Too bad," Steven said. "I was sort of looking forward to the wedding."

His bantering tone kept Lara from responding the way she wanted to, by throwing herself into his arms and agreeing to marry him at the first possible moment. Instead, she said in her sassiest manner, "Give me a proper proposal, and we'll see what we can work out."

She didn't wait to see if that proposal was forthcoming. For all of his attentiveness in the past, he had never once suggested that they marry. He had talked of a future together. He had even gone so far as to discuss their house, to think of taking her away with him. But the subject of making a permanent commitment had been skirted with surprising agility. She saw no reason to expect that had changed, and for the moment it didn't matter. He was back in her life, and that was more than enough.

Lara leaped from the warm bed before she could be caught by Steven's outstretched hand and pulled back into an embrace from which there would be no escaping.

Unperturbed by her rejection, Steven boldly followed her into the shower where he made a very tempting, seductively murmured offer to scrub her back. That delayed their departure to the farm by an hour. When they finally got downstairs, Jennifer was practically dancing around the room in impatience.

"You took forever, Aunt Lara," she chided.

"Sorry, sweet pea. We're ready now."

Jennifer regarded Steven eagerly. "Are you coming, too?"

"You bet I am," he said.

"He saved your sister," Lara reminded her. "Of course, he wants to see how she's doing."

"Oh boy, then let's hurry, Aunt Lara. I want Mr. Drake to meet my mommy and daddy, too." She bounded down the lane ahead of them, turning repeatedly to urge them to hurry. Lara caught her excitement and found herself tugging on Steven's hand.

But once the farmhouse was in sight and Lara could hear the angry voices all the way across the yard, her anticipation turned to dread. A heated exchange between her brother and sister-in-law would have been distressing enough under any circumstances, but it was especially so because she obviously was the subject of this one. She clung more tightly to Steven's hand. She suddenly wanted to take Jennifer and turn back, but it was too late. It would be cowardly to run, and there was no point to it.

"Stay out of it, Megan!" Tommy snapped, his voice carrying clearly. "I don't trust Drake. You weren't here when it happened. You don't know what that man did to her. He very nearly destroyed her. He's obviously the kind of man who gets his kicks from going around seducing women and then walking out on them."

Lara gazed at Steven in mute apology.

"He's only saying what he feels," Steven said. "I can't condemn him for that. Besides, it's true. I did hurt you terribly."

"Yes, but that's in the past. My God, you just saved his child. He should at least give you—" Before she could complete the thought, Megan's equally furious voice cut through the air.

"I think you're misjudging him. I see what he's doing for Lara now. Didn't you see how they looked at each other last night? He loves her and she loves him. If you'd really wanted to help her, you'd have spent the last years trying to get them back together, instead of encouraging her anger."

"She had every right to be angry."

"Of course, she did. But it didn't give her a moment's satisfaction, did it? Can't you be glad that she's finally happy? For the first time since you brought me here to live when we got married, your sister actually seems ready to live life again. If you can't be support-ive, you're the one who ought to stay out of it."

Jennifer turned a distraught face up to Lara. "Why are Mommy and Daddy fighting?"

"It's just a disagreement, baby," she said, then set her chin at a defiant tilt. "And I think it's just about time it ended."

Lara threw open the screen door and marched into the kitchen. Tommy and Megan glanced up guiltily, their faces flushed.

"Enough!" Lara declared. "I will not have the two of you fighting over the way I live my life." She faced Tommy and said more gently, "It is my life, you know. I have the right to make this choice, whether you approve or not."

Tommy's gaze went from her to Steven and back again. Finally his angry expression relaxed, and some of the tension went out of his shoulders. "I just don't want you to be hurt again, Sis."

"It won't happen, Tommy," Steven said, drawing the younger man's attention. He put an arm possessively around Lara's waist. "I've done my best to explain to Lara what happened back then, and she's accepted my word. I'm back in her life to stay this time, if she'll have me."

Lara waited with bated breath as Tommy absorbed this declaration from a man he'd once admired, but come to distrust. He gave Lara an intense perusal. "You're really happy, Sis? When we left here a few weeks ago, you wouldn't even go within a hundred yards of his property line. Do you actually trust him now?"

"He saved Kelly," she said simply. "He was there for me all through that. How could I not trust him? Besides, even though I fought admitting it, this is what I always wanted. Even Megan could see that."

Tommy scanned her face in that slow, assessing way of his, then nodded. "Then I guess I'll have to accept it."

He shot a warning glance at Steven, but the gaze was returned evenly. Message sent and received. Finally he held out his hand. "I hope things work out this time."

"I'm going to do my best," Steven promised.

"Now," Megan said cheerfully, "I want to see my baby who's been hiding over there behind her Aunt Lara. Come give me a hug, Jennifer."

Jennifer ran into her mother's arms, then went to sit on her father's lap while Megan and Lara fixed a huge, farm-style breakfast of eggs, bacon, home fries and fluffy biscuits. When the food was nearly ready, Megan went and got Kelly, and the whole family sat down to eat.

Lara looked around the table and felt an abiding gratitude for the blessing of their togetherness. Only Greg was missing, and he had promised to drive up from Columbus in time for lunch, so that he could see Megan and Tommy before they left again for Kansas City. Steven caught her eye and smiled, a slow, tender smile filled with understanding and promise. Her heart felt as though it might burst with happiness.

There was a tap on the back door.

"Logan," Lara called. "Come on in and grab some coffee. Would you like breakfast?"

"No, thanks, Ms. Danvers. I just wanted to get a look at the little one and see how she's doing."

"I fine," Kelly announced, still basking in her role as the center of attention. "Only one boo-boo." She pointed to the bright blue-and-white Band-Aid on her arm. "See."

"My goodness," Logan said with a shake of his head. "That's a very impressive injury."

Kelly nodded seriously. "It get better. Mommy kissed it."

"Yes, indeed. That's the very best medicine," Logan concurred. Then he glanced sideways at Tommy and suggested, "Thought maybe you'd like to take a look around, long as you're here. The corn's doing mighty well this year." The idea was presented with studied nonchalance, but Lara had the feeling it was anything but idle.

"I'd love to see it, Logan. Sis, you want to come along?"

Though Tommy's enthusiasm seemed sincere, Lara couldn't help but recall their arguments about the farm before he and Megan had left. Was he looking forward to this tour as a chance to reinforce his position that the time had come for her to sell the farm? Since she'd told Logan about Tommy's attitude, had he suggested the survey in the hopes of changing Tommy's mind? Whatever the case, she had every intention of going along to show Tommy just how smoothly things were running without him around to back up her decisions.

"Absolutely," she said. "I love showing this place off. What about the rest of you? Anyone else want to come?"

Jennifer and Kelly immediately raced for the door. Steven leaned over and kissed Lara on the cheek. "Mind if I stick around here? I'll help Megan clean up."

Steven saw that Lara was puzzled by his choice, but she accepted it readily. "See you soon, then."

When everyone else had gone, Megan poured them both another cup of coffee.

"I heard you standing up for me earlier," Steven said. "I appreciate it. I also want to thank you for asking me to look out for the girls. It forced me to do something I should have done long ago."

"Don't make me regret it," Megan replied with a fierceness that surprised him. Then she grinned. "Sorry. I guess Tommy's not the only protective member of the family. Will you marry her?"

He was startled by the blunt question but found himself grinning back at her. He had a feeling that for all of her quiet manner and amenable ways, Megan Danvers had a lot of fight in her. The straightforward query and her earlier argument with her husband were proof enough of that.

"I haven't asked her yet."

She frowned. "That sounds suspiciously like an evasion."

"I suppose it is. We're still a long way from having things resolved between us."

"Don't wait too long," she pleaded. "She's going to need you, now more than ever."

He was puzzled by her intensity. "Why?"

She seemed to hesitate, then asked slowly, "How much do you know about the past eleven years?"

"Only what she's told me, which isn't much, and what I've been able to piece together from the town gossip. It can't have been easy for her."

"Well, there are things I don't fully understand, especially about those years right after you left her, but I gather that Lara was devastated, though she fought hard not to show it. Maybe if she'd allowed herself to grieve, it would have helped. Instead, she threw herself into her studies to the exclusion of everything else. Nothing mattered to her except becoming a doctor. Then her father died. You probably know how close they were. She adored him. Still, I think she might have weathered even that, but then her mother died, too.''

''It must have been a horrible time for her. I wish to God I'd been here.''

''So do I. Maybe then she wouldn't have become so bitter and withdrawn. From what Tommy's told me, she dropped out of school without so much as a word of complaint and came back here to take charge. He and Greg were never allowed to mention college or medicine to her again. She threw herself heart and soul into making this farm work. She gave Tommy and Greg the chance to go off on their own, practically forced them to do it, from what I understand.

''When Tommy graduated from college and we got married, we came here to help. I saw how she resented your buying part of her land, but I have to tell you it was a godsend. The strain was killing her. The minute the farm was out of danger, she started encouraging us to get out on our own, to live the life we'd always wanted. Greg never came back. He's already had a one-man show down in Columbus, and there's even talk of him having an exhibit in New York. She's terribly proud of him.''

Megan looked him straight in the eye. ''I guess what I'm trying to say is that Lara is the most unselfish woman I have ever known. It's time she started doing the things she wanted to do. Maybe it's even time she got rid of this place and went back to school. That's what Tommy thinks. If I have one regret, it's that Tommy and I are going so far away. When we're gone, she'll be alone here. The prospect terrifies me. After all she's done for the rest of us, she doesn't deserve that kind of loneliness."

He understood her point at last. "I'll be here," he promised. "She won't be alone. As for choosing between the farm and medicine, that's something only she can do."

Megan nodded, then gave him a radiant smile. "I think you'll be good for her."

"God knows, I'm going to try."

"There's something else." She fumbled nervously with her spoon, picking it up, putting it down, stirring her coffee again. The sudden shift in her demeanor worried him, and he waited with an odd sense of dread to hear what was upsetting her. Finally she said, "We want to take the girls back with us when we leave today."

Steven closed his eyes and sighed. "I see."

"How do you think she'll take it?"

He responded honestly. "She's going to think you blame her for Kelly's accident."

This time it was Megan who sighed. "That's what I told Tommy." She stared at him, beseeching him to understand, but Steven felt a knife twisting in his heart on Lara's behalf. She was going to be devastated. "It's not that, you know. I swear it. It just makes sense, now that we're here, to take them back. We have the house now. Tommy's settled in his new job. He thinks it's crazy to make another trip in just a few weeks. And after all this strain, well, we just want our children with us."

"I see your point."

"Will Lara?"

"You said yourself that she's unselfish. She'll try to understand, but she's going to be hurt. There's no getting around that."

"Then I'm especially glad you two have found each other again. Maybe it'll make the pain a little more bearable."

"Let me tell her, Megan."

"To be honest, I'd be relieved if you would."

With so much on his mind, Steven had little to say as he and Megan cleaned up the kitchen. When they were done, he went outside to watch for Lara. How on earth was he going to tell her this, after all she'd been through? He was filled with frustration, yet he understood Tommy's decision. But he wondered if any of them knew just how deeply Lara's hurt was likely to run. Hopefully she wouldn't respond to this loss by withdrawing into a protective shell as she had in the past.

He was waiting by the gate when she came into view. Her blond hair sparkled in the sunlight, as if it were covered with a scattering of tiny diamonds. Her step was light, her expression gloriously happy. She came straight to him, slid an arm around his waist and placed a kiss on his cheek. Her exuberance and lack of restraint brought a smile to his lips. Her old spirit was slowly coming back.

"Miss me?" she inquired.

"Forever."

She studied him closely and apparently saw beyond the smile. "Are you sad about something?"

He held her hand, rubbing his thumb across the knuckles, then lifting it to his lips. He kissed the callused tips of her fingers. "We need to talk."

She was instantly alert. "What about?"

"Come. Let's sit on the porch."

Her eyes widened, and her hand tightened around his. "Steven, what is it? Something's wrong, isn't it? Is it Kelly? Is there some aftereffect from her fall?"

"No," he said promptly, furious with himself for frightening her. "Not the way you mean."

"Then what?"

He struggled to find the right words. "You know, this trip was an unexpected expense for Megan and Tommy," he began finally. "With a new job and the move, they can't have a lot of extra money right now."

"Good heavens, is that all?" she said, her relief painfully obvious. "I hadn't even thought about that. It's no problem. I have a little money put away. I'll pay for their tickets."

He touched a finger to her lips. Her quick, typically giving response wrenched his heart. "No, love. That's not the point. If it was merely a question of money, I could loan it to them. There's been the time away from their new home, too."

"What are you getting at?" Then a suspicion apparently popped into her mind, and her voice went flat. "They want to take the girls back with them, don't they?"

Steven put a hand against her cheek and met her distraught gaze. Her eyes grew misty when he nodded.

"It's because of what . . ."

He gathered her close until he could feel the dull pounding of her heart. So slow now, the joyous beating he'd inspired during the night stilled by her pain. She smelled of sunshine and hay and a lingering trace of some light, flowery scent.

"Hush," he said gently. "Don't even think that way. I told you why. It has nothing at all to do with what happened to Kelly. They just feel that as long as they're here, it makes sense for Jennifer and Kelly to leave with them now."

"Oh, Steven," she whispered, resting her cheek against his chest. He stroked her head, his fingers tangling in the silken strands of her hair. "What am I going to do?"

"You're going to say goodbye and promise that you'll come to Kansas City very soon to visit."

"But then what?"

"Then you and I will start talking about making a life for ourselves." He hesitated. "If that's what you want."

A sigh whispered across his chest, and she lifted her face until she could look into his eyes. "Thank you."

"For what?"

"For making this easier to bear."

Though Steven was grateful that she felt that way, he wasn't so sure it was true. The afternoon was clearly a torment for her. She went upstairs and helped Megan pack the girls' clothes and toys. He stood in the doorway of the room and watched as she hugged Kelly's ragged bear tightly before placing it ever so carefully in a carry-on bag. Her expression grew sadder with each passing moment, and though she said nothing to make Tommy and Megan feel guilty, there was no doubt in anyone's mind that she was falling apart inside.

Even Greg's arrival didn't cheer her. If anything, his determined rambunctiousness and ready wit made her gloom seem all the more pronounced. In the end it was Greg who drove Megan and Tommy and the girls to the airport in Toledo. Biting her trembling lower lip and blinking back tears, Lara insisted on saying her goodbyes at the farm. She stood on the front porch and waved until the car was out of sight.

Then she turned and with a tiny cry of dismay buried her face against Steven's chest and sobbed as though her heart had broken.

"Shh, sweetheart. It's okay. You'll see them again soon. Shh."

Witnessing her desolation now gave Steven a tangible image of what his own departure must have cost her. So many goodbyes for such a young lifetime, he thought. It was all he could do to keep from weeping with her.

Eight

The rain began after midnight. Lara heard it pounding rhythmically on the tin roof and felt it was a fitting accompaniment for the dull throbbing in her head and the heaviness in her heart. She had anticipated with dread the time when Jennifer and Kelly would leave, but she had thought she could prepare herself for it. Unfortunately it had taken her by surprise, before she could muster her strength to face it well. Only Steven's presence had kept her from crawling into bed and drowning in her misery.

She rolled over and caught him looking at her.

"Can't sleep?"

She shook her head.

"Let me rub your back. Maybe you'll relax."

She turned onto her stomach and felt the bed shift as Steven knelt over her. His hands touched her bare shoulders, and she again felt the sharp shock of desire sweep through her. But he began kneading the muscles, conscious only of her tension. She sighed with a sense of regret and tried to make her mind a blank, to let the soothing sensations wash over her.

Instead, she kept seeing Jennifer and Kelly waving excitedly to her from the back seat of Greg's car. They were so caught up in the adventure ahead of them, they hadn't shed a single tear for what they were leaving behind. Not for the farm. Not for Logan. Not for her.

"Stop dwelling on it," Steven said, as if he could read her mind.

"What makes you think I'm thinking about the kids?"

"Because these knotted muscles of yours are getting worse, not better, and I don't think my technique's at fault."

She smiled into the pillow. "Sorry if I'm destroying your ego."

"Forget my ego. I'm talking about your sense of loss. You're letting it get all out of proportion. Sweetheart, this isn't forever. You can visit Jennifer and Kelly. They'll probably be back for Christmas and again next summer. And there is one positive benefit you're ignoring completely."

"What's that?"

"This." He dropped a kiss on her shoulder. It sent yet another predictable tingle dancing down her spine as he added, "You and I would not be able to be together quite so easily with your watchful little nieces around."

Grateful for his understanding and his ardent caring, she rolled over and drew his head down until his lips hovered just above hers. Her eyes met his, searching for and finding the gleam of desire that warmed them to the deepest blue. "How did you come up with the one thing that might cheer me up?"

He gave her a crooked grin. "Actually, it was no more than wishful thinking. I was hoping that you felt the same way about this that I do. I don't ever want us to be separated again."

He closed the infinitesimal distance between them then, his lips claiming hers with such absolute tenderness that it took her breath away. Then with unending gentleness he swept her away to their own private island of dreams, where magic caressed her flesh and brought her a blessed relief from the anguish of her thoughts.

At last, Steven's arms around her, she slept.

In the morning, though, her depression returned, magnified by the rolling clouds that masked the sun and threatened yet more rain. Steven found her at the kitchen table, a cup of coffee clasped in both hands, staring off into the distance. He brushed a kiss across her forehead.

"What shall we do today?" he asked, his attitude determinedly upbeat.

She faced him guiltily. "Would you mind if I go out and help Logan with the harvesting? Maybe the exercise will help me shake off this rotten mood. There's no point in subjecting you to it."

"I'm not complaining."

She gave him a wavery smile. "No, you're not. How did I ever get to be so lucky?"

"You weren't saying that about me a couple of weeks ago. You were calling me the worst sort of beast then."

"You've changed," she replied, then shook her head. "No. I'm the one who's changed. Hell, maybe neither one of us has changed. I don't know."

She put her cup down so hard the coffee splattered across the table. She ignored it. "I've got to get out of here."

She started for the door, then turned back and asked hesitantly, "Will I see you later?"

"Why don't we get away from here, maybe go out for dinner and a movie?"

Lara nodded unenthusiastically. As long as they were together, what they did hardly mattered. Nothing mattered, she thought dismally.

"Fine," she said, and left, refusing to think about the confused look in his eyes, the worried frown on his brow.

She hadn't gone ten yards when she realized how impossible she was being. She was not going to sulk forever. She'd snap herself out of this. In the meantime she went back to the kitchen and gave Steven the lingering, breath-stealing kiss he deserved. "I'm sorry. I'll try to be in a better mood by tonight."

"No problem," he said, forgiving her so readily it made her heart ache at even the momentary unhappiness she'd caused him.

"If you're not," he added, "I'll just have to dream up some extraordinary means of cheering you up."

Despite the promise of an enjoyable evening ahead of her, her day went from bad to worse. She was so distracted that Logan finally ordered her away from the equipment. "The mood you're in, you're downright dangerous out here. If you don't hurt yourself, you're likely to ruin half the crop. Get away for a bit. Go for a walk. Go for a swim. We can manage without you."

She knew he was right, but the dismissal did nothing to improve that awful feeling of being abandoned and useless. If anything, it compounded it. She wasn't even needed on her own farm anymore.

She walked down to the stream, kicked off her shoes and waded along the edge but couldn't seem to work up the energy to go for a swim. When she tired of that, she went back to the house, made a pitcher of lemonade and took a glass out to the front porch, letting the self-pity build until it threatened to engulf her. In all her life it was something she had rarely permitted, but this time she wasn't sure she had the will to fight it off.

The sky grew darker, the air oppressively still. Finally the ominous signs registered.

"Oh, dear heaven," she said softly. She ran inside to tune the radio to a weather channel. As she expected, they were announcing the sightings of tornadoes and warning residents in the area to take cover at the first sign of one of the dangerous funnel clouds.

Surely Logan and the others had left the fields by now, she thought, then decided she couldn't take any chances. She would have to warn them. Wrapping herself in a yellow waterproof cape, she ran along the

track to the field where she had left Logan. Fat drops
of rain began to fall, scattered at first and then with
more insistency. Long before the men were in sight,
her hair was drenched, her shoes soaked through and
caked with mud.

"Logan!" she shouted as soon as she thought her
voice would carry to him. "Get the equipment inside.
Tornadoes have been sighted."

He waved her back. "I just want to get this last little bit harvested before the storm breaks, Ms. Danvers. Shouldn't take more than another ten, maybe
fifteen minutes."

"Don't risk it. A few rows of corn aren't worth it."

"You get on back to the house. I'll have everything
back in the barn before you know it."

"Logan!"

"Go on, missy. We're not going to lose this corn."

"Then I'm staying to help. It's my responsibility."

He scowled at her. "We don't need your help.
There's no sense all of us staying out here getting wet-
ter than a bunch of ducks. While you and I stand here
arguing, I could be finishing up."

Lara reluctantly gave in and started back to the
house. She was barely at the edge of the field when she
heard the loud roar that could have been a train rattling along nearby tracks. But there was no railroad,
and she knew well what the ominous sound meant.
She whirled around and scanned the sky and found
exactly what she feared: a huge, dark funnel cloud,
twirling debris up from the land. Where it skimmed
the earth, it was a tight, black column. But as it

reached toward the sky, it expanded into a wide swirl that dipped and swayed like some evil prankster.

"Dear God," she breathed in horrified fascination, unable to tear her gaze away from the tornado's relentless path toward her. At last she came to her senses, recalling that she should be inside, away from glass. Terrified now, she raced through the house to the storm cellar. She flipped on the cellar lights, but they flickered, then died as the sound of the approaching tornado increased to ear-shattering levels. Without taking the time to search for a flashlight, she felt her way down the stairs.

In the basement she found a stack of old blankets and sat down. She drew her knees up to her chest and wrapped her arms around them and waited, her pulse beating erratically. What little light penetrated the darkness from the two high windows on the opposite side of the room began to fade until the room was pitch black. The whole earth seemed to tremble then. The house creaked on its foundation. And a deep shudder swept through Lara.

She had seen tornadoes before, witnessed the aftermath of their wild fury, but never had she been caught in the middle of one. Never had she known this choking fear that came from having her own fate wrested from her control by a willful force of nature. She could do nothing to hold back the inevitable destruction, nothing even to lessen it. She could only pray.

She thanked God that Jennifer and Kelly were not here to suffer this agonizing torment of waiting for whatever might strike. She prayed desperately that Steven was someplace safe and secure, that Logan and the men had reached the relative safety of the barn. And she prayed that she would survive to experience once more the depth of Steven's love. She wouldn't be defeated by everything that had happened. She would, rather, fight for a better future. With Steven back in her life, happiness was finally within her grasp. She suffered another pang of regret that she had allowed her black mood to spoil even one moment of their time together.

The terrible sound of the storm rumbled on. Rain continued to lash the house, whipping branches from the trees and throwing them against the roof. Still she waited, knowing that until the storm's fury fully abated the danger was not past. She saw occasional flashes of lightning through the windows, heard echoing cracks of thunder. There was another rumbling at a distance, then another. Perhaps it was only thunder, but it was frightening nonetheless. Each one seemed to wrench her insides, leaving her cold and shivering. Her imagination ran wild, taking up where reality left off. She fought against wasted tears, knowing there wouldn't be a moment's peace for her until she could see for herself that Steven and the others had survived.

And the farm. What damage was it suffering? Would there even be corn left to harvest once the storm had its way? Would the debt she had struggled so long and hard to reduce mount again with no crops to meet the loan payment?

Suddenly it was all too much for her. The emotional intensity of the last week caught up with her, and tears began to spill down her cheeks. Angrily she brushed them away, but more followed.

She'd thought she was so damned independent, that she didn't need anyone. For years now she'd managed her life, this farm, but she realized now that's all it had been: managing. She'd done what was expected of her, but she hadn't been fulfilled and happy. She'd been out to prove herself, perhaps even hoping to show Steven how little his betrayal had affected her.

What a sham! In no more than a few days he'd shown her exactly how much she still needed him to fire her senses, to share her successes, simply to care. She was strong. She'd had to be. She knew now that she could survive anything. But she was not so strong that she didn't require love. No one was ever that independent.

Her tears spent at last, she got up and went over to one of the high windows to see what was happening outside. She pulled over a chair and stepped up on it. Just as she did, there was another explosion of sound, the shattering of glass and then...nothing.

Steven had been in his study when the storm broke. He tried calling Lara as soon as he heard the tornado warnings, but the phone lines were already down. His first instinct had been to drive to the farm, but Mrs. Marston had stopped him at the front door.

"You won't do that girl a bit of good if your car is picked up, turned on its roof and set down in the next county," she scolded. "Now don't you go being foolish, Mr. Drake. You built that fancy storm cellar downstairs just for an occasion like this. Get on down there, and I'll make you a pot of tea, and we can wait this out."

He saw the wisdom in her advice, but he chafed at the waiting. He paced the cellar, listening to the wrath of the wind, his muscles knotted in frustration. When Mrs. Marston offered him tea, he growled at her.

"What if she's out in the fields and can't get back?"

"That girl has lived in these parts a whole lot longer than you have. She knows all about these storms. I'm sure she's not taking any chances."

"You're very calm about this," he accused.

"No point in getting myself all riled up. There's not a thing you or I can do to stop whatever's going to happen."

"I'm not sure I'm in the mood to discuss your fatalistic approach to life. I'd rather be doing something."

He caught her grinning at him, though she took a quick swallow of tea to cover it. "Why don't you put up those shelving units you bought, as long as you're down here?"

He gave her a fierce scowl.

"Well, it was just an idea," she huffed right back at him.

He took up pacing again, his nerves tightening with each crash of thunder. When one of the basement windows was shattered by a storm-tossed tree branch, he whirled around and headed for the steps.

"That does it! I'm going after her. She could be in danger over there."

When Mrs. Marston opened her mouth to protest, he held up his hand. "Save it. I'm going. I'll take the car. Despite your dire prediction that I'll end up like Dorothy in *The Wizard of Oz*, I think the car should give me some protection.''

The housekeeper rolled her eyes heavenward, but she kept silent as he ran up the stairs.

He didn't stop for a raincoat. His clothes were soaked through by the time he reached the car. The eerie stillness that usually preceded the worst part of this kind of weather system had been replaced by an old-fashioned beauty of a storm.

As he drove along the winding road that led from his house to the entrance to the Danvers' farm, his eyes widened in incredulity. While there had been a few broken branches scattered about his own property, there had been nothing to suggest the devastation he found as he drove past Lara's fields. A wide, tangled path of destruction had been cut through the middle, leaving raw earth and broken stalks in its wake. A mighty oak tree, its trunk three feet or more in diameter, had been twisted from the ground and left sprawling across dangling power lines. Tree limbs and debris were everywhere.

With the road blocked by the fallen tree, Steven pulled onto the shoulder and, being careful of the dangerous electrical wires, left the car and set off on foot.

His heart hammered with fear as he made his way through the destroyed field. Was this where Lara had been working this morning? Had she made it back to the house? Or had she stubbornly refused to take shelter, hoping to salvage one more bushel of corn, before the storm broke around her? He began to run, oblivious to the mud that sucked at his shoes and the rain that pounded down.

As he reached the barn, Logan called out to him.

"Is Lara with you?" Steven called back, his words whipped around by the wind.

"No. I sent her back early. She's probably pacing around the storm cellar."

Logan paused, as if trying to work up the courage to say something more. He took off his Stetson and fiddled with it, turning it around and around in his weathered hands. Steven found himself growing impatient. Finally, brown eyes filled with dismay turned on him.

"Mr. Drake, I'm worried about how she's gonna take this." He gestured toward the fields. "She's bound to be mighty upset when she sees what's happened here. She was counting on this harvest."

The foreman's concern confirmed his own fears. "I know that, Logan. How bad is it?"

"Can't say for sure. I haven't been around the whole place, but from what I seen so far, it looks pretty bad."

Steven sighed. "That's what I was afraid of. I cut through the northwestern field coming over here. It's like it's been mowed down. I've never seen anything like it."

Logan shook his head. "I've seen it all too often. It's the kinda thing that near wiped her daddy out more than once."

Steven heard the genuine affection and anxiety in Logan's voice and patted the older man on the shoulder. "She's going to need your help more than ever now. Why don't I go find her, and we can ride around the fields together and see just how bad this is?''

Logan shoved his hat back on his head and nodded. ''I'll be waiting right here, Mr. Drake. Ain't no use hurryin' now.''

Steven walked slowly to the house, every beat of his heart painful. He wrestled with the desire to pack a suitcase, sweep Lara into his arms and whisk her off to some magical place where the problems of the farm would seem far removed and unimportant, but he knew that such a place did not exist. For all that she'd hated it as a girl, for all that it had demanded of her, she loved the farm. She would fight his protective instincts, if that's what it took to save it. He was proud of her gutsy determination, respected her for the way she'd handled tough times. No, she probably wouldn't appreciate his butting in and trying to protect her. All he could do was try to help in any way she'd let him.

When he reached the back door of the house, he called out to her. The shout echoed back to him, but there was no response.

''Lara,'' he called again, struck by the faintest sense of unease. There was no sign of her. ''Lara!''

Choking back a terrible sense of panic, he found the door to the basement. He threw it open and stared down into pitch darkness. He hunted through kitchen drawers until he found a candle, and when it was lit, he began his descent, heart hammering.

''Lara!''

His call was greeted by a deathly silence. The candle cast flickering light for only a few feet around him. As he moved on, fighting shadows, a hard knot of fear formed in his stomach. He was halfway around the room, when he saw her lying in a crumpled heap on the floor, rain pouring in on her through the broken window.

He was at her side in an instant, his heart in his throat. "Lara," he said softly. "Sweetheart, can you hear me?"

When he went to brush the hair from her face, his hand came away sticky with blood. "Oh, my God," he murmured. "Lara!"

Gently he felt her head, locating the huge bump just over her temple, then the cut along her cheek. She'd apparently been slashed by the broken glass, besides being hit by whatever had flown through the window. He felt for her pulse. It was weak but steady, and the flow of blood from the wound seemed to have slowed. Not wanting to leave her to go in search of a washcloth, he took off his shirt and ripped it, then held a strip of the cloth against the injury.

"Come on, sweetheart, wake up. This is no time to be taking a nap."

Her eyelashes fluttered against her cheeks.

"That's the way. You can do it. Wake up for me."

After what seemed an eternity, her eyes blinked open.

"Steven, is that you?" Lara responded sleepily. She saw the flickering candlelight, then heard his heavy sigh of relief. "Is the storm over?"

"The worst of it is. How do you feel?"

She tried to sit up, winced at the sudden pounding in her head and lay back. She touched her fingers to her temple. "Why does my head hurt?"

"Apparently a branch or something blew in through the window and knocked you out." She could see the anxiety in his eyes, the tension in his brow.

"You've been crying," she said, her thumb rubbing gently across the telltale traces on his cheeks. "Are you okay? You aren't hurt, are you?"

He laughed. "No, sweetheart, I'm not the one who's hurt. I almost went crazy, though, when I realized the phone lines were down and I couldn't check on you. Then when I got over here and couldn't find you, it scared the daylights out of me."

She put her hand over his. "I'm fine."

"We'll let a doctor be the judge of that."

"No doctor," she insisted, forcing herself to sit up. "The headache should go away soon, and I have to see how things are around here. The tornadoes sounded so close. Did they touch down?"

The question was greeted by silence.

"Steven?" She scanned his eyes for the truth he couldn't seem to say. "They did a lot of damage, didn't they? Have you seen Logan?"

"He's fine. He's waiting for you outside."

"And the fields?" When he didn't respond, she demanded, "Dammit, tell me, Steven. I need to know. I'd rather hear it from you before I see for myself." The pounding in her head intensified. She closed her eyes against the pain, and her hand flew up instinctively to touch the injury.

Steven apparently saw that his silence was only increasing her agitation. The stubborn gleam in his eyes faded. He sighed wearily. "I've only seen one field. It was pretty badly damaged. I don't know about the rest."

"I have to see."

"Not yet," he said. "There's the little matter of your clothes that got soaked in the rain and the bump on your head to consider. I'll make you a deal."

One eyebrow lifted fractionally. "Yes?"

"We'll go upstairs. I'll check this out in a better light, and then, *if it looks okay*, you can change, and we'll go out and see the farm."

"Is there an alternative?"

"Sure." He grinned at her wickedly. "We go straight to the hospital."

She frowned at him. "I'll take the deal."

He nodded in satisfaction. "I thought you might."

The next thing she knew, she was in his arms being carried up the basement stairs. "This is getting to be a habit," she noted. "Be careful. If I get used to it, you may have to carry me everywhere."

"It could be arranged," he said as he settled her into a kitchen chair. "Where is your first-aid kit?"

"There's one in the bathroom cupboard."

As soon as he was gone, she was tempted to make a run for it, but common sense—and the unrelenting pounding in her head—kept her still. He was back before she could give the matter a second thought.

"I'm surprised," he said. "I thought you'd be halfway out the door by now."

"Believe me, I thought about it."

"What stopped you?"

"Knowing that Logan would just haul me right back in here to you."

"Sensible girl. Now let me take a look at your head."

She winced as he washed away the blood.

"Good. Looks like there's no glass in here." He put a liberal amount of antiseptic on the wound, holding her head still.

"Are you sure you're not enjoying this?" she grumbled, glaring at him. Then she saw her own pain reflected in his eyes. "Sorry."

His finger trailed lazily down her cheek. "No problem."

Lara sighed. "I'm scared," she admitted, her voice shaky. Her heart seemed to weigh more heavily than ever in her chest. She hadn't thought it possible that she could feel this weary, this drained of emotion. How much more could she possibly take? Steven seemed to sense her dismay, because he put aside the first-aid materials and drew her into his arms.

"Whatever it takes, we'll handle this together," he promised. "You're not alone anymore."

His words, rather than reassuring her as he meant them to, only convinced her that the damage must be incredibly bad. If that was so, his promise might be the only thing that could keep her going.

Nine

Lara's hands were shaking, and there was a sick feeling in the pit of her stomach as she and Steven approached the back door. She gazed up at him in mute appeal. He gave her an encouraging smile and squeezed her hand.

"Together," he reminded her.

It gave her the strength to open the door and walk outside. And then her heart seemed to stop. Her hand closed urgently on Steven's forearm. The look she gave him was stricken.

All around her was chaos. A screen, apparently ripped from one of the windows—or perhaps even from some other house—lay twisted at the base of a tree. Bits of unidentifiable metal, pieces of farm machinery, no doubt, glinted in the sunlight that was breaking through the clouds. A few broken tree limbs dangled by one last strip of wood, while others had been tossed around like so many pick-up-sticks. The shrubs along one side of the house had been uprooted and were scattered in every direction. Two windows in addition to the one in the basement were in jagged pieces. Debris and dirt clung to the white paint, giving the house an untended appearance. A child's tricycle she'd never seen before was half buried in the mud.

Lara swallowed hard as Logan hurried toward her. His expression grew worried as he spotted her injuries.

"You okay, Ms. Danvers?"

"I'm fine. How are the rest of the men?"

"They're okay. We got everything we could into the barn before the worst of it hit. I've sent 'em on home now to check on their families. They'll be back, though, to help with the cleanup."

"How'd the cows and horses do?"

"Better 'n some of the men," he said with a lopsided grin. "The horses got a little nervous, pranced around in their stalls some. Bessie's got a scrape on her rump from bumping into the side of her stall, but that's the only injury as far as I can tell. You ready to go out and take a look at things?"

She glanced up at Steven, and his grip on her hand tightened. She gave Logan a jaunty smile, determined to make the best of whatever hand fate had dealt her. "Let's do it. I'm as ready as I'll ever be."

"Come on then. I've saddled the horses."

"I'm not sure about riding the horses, Logan," Steven said. "Not with her head injury."

"Of course not. I'll get the pickup."

"We won't be able to get around in the truck," Lara protested. "There are too many trees down."

"But—"

"Steven, I'll be okay. If my head starts to bother me, I promise we'll turn back."

He didn't look pleased, but he gave in.

They began their ride with the northwestern field Steven had seen on his way over. Lara had to choke back a cry of dismay when she saw that very little of the fine, healthy crop was left standing. A mat of twisted green stalks covered the sea of mud. Only a few rows in one corner had survived unscathed.

They rode on. As they guided the horses carefully around the scattered debris and fallen wires, Lara felt her determination begin to flag. It was far worse than she'd anticipated. Not a single field had been left untouched except, ironically, the one they had just harvested. When she saw that, she almost sobbed. It was the cruelest twist of all.

"Can we save any of this?" she asked Logan, her heart heavy, her expression hopeless.

He shoved his hat to the back of his head and regarded her sympathetically. "Hard to say, Ms. Danvers. I suppose it's possible that some of the corn could be replanted, if the roots aren't damaged. No telling if they'll take hold, though. Some of this may be okay for feed. When the men get back, we'll start doing what we can."

"Thanks, Logan." She took a deep breath. "I suppose once you've finished cleaning up, we'd better pay the men off and let them go. There's not enough of a crop to justify keeping them till the fall. You and I can handle what there is.''

"I hate to say it, missy, but I think you're right. I'm real sorry, ma'am.''

"Thanks, Logan.''

Steven had remained silent throughout the exchange, but as they rode back to the barn alone, he said, "This is going to make things rough for you, isn't it?''

"It's going to put me back at Mr. Hogan's mercy, if that's what you mean. I have enough to live on and to pay Logan, but I'll probably have to ask for an extension on the loan on the farm, and I'll need to borrow money for next year's seed.'' She bit her lip to keep from crying out in frustration as the harsh impact of the tornado's work sank in. She tried to hide her mounting distress with a nonchalant shrug. "Hey, this is just one of the hazards of farming, right? I should be used to it. It happened to my father often enough.''

She swung down from the saddle and straight into Steven's arms. They encircled her waist and held her in place. He gazed at her with piercing intensity. "Don't give me that unconcerned act, Lara. I know this is killing you.''

She glared up at him, wrestling with her emotions. She lost.

"All right,'' she exploded suddenly, all of her anger at the injustice of it spilling out. She spun from his embrace. "I hate it! I hate being beholden to the bank again. I hate knowing that no matter how well I run this place year after year, it takes one short storm to destroy it. I hate living on the edge, never being able to get ahead.''

She began pacing so furiously that it made the horses jittery. Finally she stopped and faced Steven again, eyes blazing.

''Do you know I actually had begun to set money aside so I could make you an offer on your land someday? I was so damn proud of that. I wanted the Danvers' property to be whole again. What's happened here today will take every cent of that savings and more.'' She waved her hand in the air in an angry gesture. ''Whoosh! A storm blows through and it's all gone. Just like that.''

''You could walk away from it,'' Steven said quietly.

Her head snapped around, and she stared at him. ''What?''

''I said you could give it all up, end the uncertainty. You could go back to school, become a doctor. That's what Megan and Tommy want for you.''

Her brow knit in a puzzled frown. ''You discussed it with them?''

''Only Megan. She's worried about you. She and Tommy only want what's best for you.''

''Is that what you think I should do? Do you think I should give this up and go back to school?''

''I didn't say that. I said it's an option. Have you considered it?''

''No,'' she said heatedly, suddenly angry at him and not entirely sure why. Perhaps it was simply that he was pushing her in a direction that had been closed to her for too long. "I gave that idea up years ago. It's too late."

"I'm not saying it wouldn't be difficult, but it's not too late." He placed his hands on her shoulders and forced her to look at him. "Think about it, Lara. What is it you really want? Don't waste your life doing something you claim to hate. If you have a different dream, you owe it to yourself to try and make it come true. I understand that for years you had obligations here, but Tommy and Greg are on their own now. The farm is an emotional, physical and financial drain. If you want out, now's the time."

She looked around and tried to imagine walking away from the farm, giving up the backbreaking work and uncertainty. She couldn't do it. "It's been in my family for generations," she protested. "I can't just leave it."

His gaze was unrelenting. "Is that your sense of duty talking or genuine caring?"

Her voice faltered, her determination suddenly less certain. "I . . . I don't know."

He tilted her chin up and smiled at her. "Think about it. Okay?"

She nodded, knowing that she would have little peace now that the subject had been raised.

He gave her a gentle nudge in the direction of the house. "Now, let's go get this place cleaned up."

They worked for hours. Steven started by making the repairs to the windows and hosing down the outside of the house, while Lara worked in the yard. A few of the shrubs were straggly but salvageable, and she put them back into place. She hauled limbs into a pile near the barn, planning to chop them later for kindling and firewood. Then she raked the debris into piles to be put into garbage bags and hauled away.

She worked with a savage intensity, needing the strain of her muscles, welcoming the exhaustion that followed. The sun, mocking them now with its brightness, beat down on her shoulders and brought sweat to her brow. At times she paused to watch Steven. The bunching of the muscles in his shoulders, the gleam of perspiration on his bare chest stirred a sharp pang of longing in her heart. She wanted him, needed him to fill this aching emptiness that had settled in her abdomen. Her pulse raced, until finally she had to look away.

By sundown the worst of the damage around the house had been cleared away. She turned the hose on and rinsed the traces of grime off her hands and face. Then she sank down on a bale of hay in the shade. She found a rubber band in her pocket and lifted her hair off of her neck into a cooler ponytail.

"Well, if it isn't Farmer Danvers," Steven taunted, coming upon her. Blue eyes glittered dangerously as he propped a dusty boot on the bale beside her. "This sight reminds me of something."

"A Norman Rockwell painting on the virtues of backbreaking labor? Or maybe *American Gothic*?"

"Definitely not *American Gothic*," he said thoughtfully. "You don't look nearly stoic enough for that."

"Then what?" she asked, her mood lifting under his gentle teasing.

"It reminds me of the way you looked that night at the stream, the night we made love for the first time." He leaned forward and ran a finger lazily along the line of her jaw as his gaze captured hers and held. "Want to go swimming?"

Lara's breath caught in her throat. Teasing shifted to a thrilling new tension. Excitement strummed across taut nerves.

"Now?" Her voice came out as a husky whisper.

Steven nodded.

Without tearing her gaze away from his, Lara held out her hand. He took it, and they headed toward the stream. With her heart thudding more wildly with each passing second, Lara thought the walk would take forever. She was hardly aware of the fallen trees and scattered branches they passed. Every nerve in her body was vibrantly attuned to the man next to her. After everything that had happened today, after all the pain she had suffered, he was still capable of reaching her heart and making it whole.

Dusk was falling as they reached the stream, and in the dim light she watched as he reached for the buttons of her blouse. His tanned fingers, the tips rougher than usual from the work they'd done, skimmed along her already burning flesh as her shirt fell open. He traced a line from the base of her throat down the delicate valley between her breasts over her ribs and on to the waistband of her jeans. Where he touched, she burned, and the rest of her skin suffered the sweet agony of waiting for his caress.

He took the band from her hair, lifting its golden weight until it settled in a cloud around her shoulders. With the gentlest of touches, he brushed back the curls that had wisped about her face.

And all the while he loved her with his eyes. Burning, sapphire-bright eyes that spoke of desire.

"You are so very beautiful," he murmured, his voice low and husky. "So very desirable. You can't imagine how many times I've thought of that night, of you here. I want you just as much now as I did then." He brought her hand to rest on his body as proof, and the rigid heat seemed to sear her.

Then the rest of her clothing fell away under his tender guidance, and his lips covered the bareness with a cloak of kisses that warmed more effectively than the glow of the sun. Liquid fire ran through her veins and weakened her knees so that she had to rest her hands on his shoulders. Shoulders that were broad and well muscled and could bear the weight of her problems along with his own. Shoulders that tempted her to disrobe him as he had her.

When he stood before her, magnificently naked, she reached out to touch him, then hesitated, awed that he was hers. Then she watched in wonder as he trembled in wait of her touch. At last her fingers were upon his chest, seeking and finding his masculine nipples, tangling in the wiry whorls of hair, then moving daringly lower to the sweetly throbbing core of his desire. He groaned in pleasure at that most intimate caress, before gathering her to him and plunging them both into the cool water of the stream.

With ripples lapping at their flesh, he settled her in place, filling her, completing her. Rocking slowly, he began a motion that was sweet torment, as he found the tip of her breast with his mouth. The ministrations of his tongue sent spirals of aching ecstasy shooting through her. Braced on the tense muscles of his shoulders, her fingers dug into his flesh as her head fell back. His lips left her breast to plunder the tender skin she'd exposed.

The past came back to her in a rush of vivid sensations. This was the way it had been for them before, yet different. The passion burned every bit as brightly, the hunger mounted with as much demand, but the climax that was rushing at them with a sense of wild abandon carried with it the knowledge that they had endured. They had overcome feelings of betrayal, separation and loneliness and found that nothing was as strong as their love for each other.

When Steven's name was torn from her lips, a hoarse cry in the night's stillness, Lara knew an instant's terror that caution could be overcome so easily. Then ecstasy followed, and the doubts were no more.

When she could find the breath to speak, Lara murmured, "We should go back. It's getting cool."

"And I'm starving," Steven admitted with a rueful laugh. "Much as I would like to stay right here and pretend the boundaries of our world go no farther, I think you're right. We should go back."

Once the decision was regretfully made, they hurried into their clothes and strolled back to the farmhouse. In the kitchen they worked in companionable silence, stopping only for stolen kisses as they chopped vegetables and grated cheese for omelets.

"We have biscuits, too," Lara announced, pulling out the package of homemade biscuits Megan had left for her in the freezer.

"The only thing missing is wine," Steven said, looking with satisfaction at the amassed ingredients for their dinner.

Lara protested. "Wine's the last thing I need. I'll fall asleep in my plate."

"That wouldn't be such a bad thing. You're exhausted. You need a good night's rest. Why don't I run home and get the wine?"

"Steven, really. I don't need it. A huge glass of iced tea will be terrific."

"Okay," he relented. "Tonight your every wish is my command." His hand rested at the base of her spine, and he turned her until he could drop a kiss on her lips. Lara felt her senses stir again, just from that simple gesture.

"You'd better not distract me," she warned. "Or you really will starve to death."

Forcing her attention back to the stove, she sautéed the vegetables, then added them to the eggs. In no time the food was on the table, and even more quickly it was gone.

"That's ridiculous," she said with a laugh, looking around at the empty plates. "There's not even a crumb left, and we ate as though we were afraid someone would come in here and steal it away from us."

"Still hungry?"

She patted her stomach. "No. I think that was just about right. What about you?"

His eyes twinkled. "There is one hunger that isn't satisfied."

"Oh, really. I thought we'd taken care of that one first."

"That was just the appetizer. I was thinking of dessert."

"Is this insatiable side to you something I need to worry about?"

"I was rather hoping you'd find it one of my better qualities," he taunted. Then his expression suddenly turned sober. "There's something we should talk about."

She waved her hands in a gesture of truce. "Please, no serious talk tonight. I just want to get some sleep."

"No. This can't wait. It's something we touched on this afternoon."

"This afternoon?"

"Yes. We were talking about your going back to school."

"Steven, I don't want to discuss that again. It's out of the question."

"Because you don't want to go?"

"I didn't say that "

"Is it the expense?"

"That's certainly part of it. There's no denying that medical school would cost a fortune. As you well know, I'm a little short on fortunes these days."

"I'm not."

Her eyes widened. "Forget it! I will not take money from you."

"Why not? Lara, I have more than enough. If college is something you want, I'd like to help you. It would make me happy to see you get all the things you deserve. God knows I owe you that much.''

''Absolutely not! You don't owe me anything. It's bad enough being in debt to the bank. I won't start borrowing money from friends.''

''Aren't I more than a friend?'' he inquired with a wry expression.

She waved aside the argument. ''Semantics. You're missing the point. If I can't do it on my own, I won't do it.''

''Does that mean you want to, though?''

''Dammit, leave it be. I didn't say that.''

A silence fell between them, and she thought that was the end of the matter, but not meeting her eyes, Steven said slowly, ''There's another alternative.''

''What?''

''Sell me the farm.''

Those four words echoed off the walls, pounding into Lara's head as violently as unexpected blows.

Sell me the farm.

Was that what all this had been about? After eleven years was Steven after nothing but her land? Betrayal, so recently dismissed as a thing of the past, came surging back to choke her on its bitterness.

Shaking, her whole body literally trembling with anger, she got to her feet. ''Get out,'' she said very, very softly.

Steven stared at her in shock. ''What?''

''You heard me. I asked you, no, I ordered you to get out of my house.''

''Lara?''

His confusion appeared real, but she was relentless. Her voice rose. "Leave! Now!"

He stayed right where he was. "Sit down. Let's talk about this. Why on earth are you so angry?"

"I think you've said quite enough. If you won't leave, I will."

Faced with her stubborn determination, he finally stood. But when he got to the door, he turned and tried one last time. "Lara," he began, his voice a plea.

She turned her back on him.

Only after she heard him leave, heard the finality of the door closing, did she give in to the sobs that seemed to well up from deep inside. Picking up a plate she flung it at the door, then cried all the harder as it shattered and fell to the floor.

The land! The damned land! That's all it had ever been about. Fool that she was, she had actually believed that he loved her, when all he really cared about were these acres she owned. She would pay him back for this. By God, she would find a way to make him pay.

Ten

———

A lacy pattern of silver and shadow covered the lawn. It was nearly dawn, and hints of pink were coloring the horizon. Lara sat sideways in the swing on the front porch, idly pushing herself back and forth with one foot. Normally it would have been just enough motion to lull her to sleep, but her mind had been churning restlessly all night, and the soothing rhythm of the swing had no effect. She finally gave up on rest and decided to simply enjoy the faint breeze and to think through this latest turn of events in her tumultuous relationship with Steven.

For hours now she had thought about his offer again and again, trying to make sense of it. It always came back to the same thing. He'd never given up on owning the Danvers' acreage. She wanted to believe that over the past few weeks there had been something lasting between them. More than once he had made a declaration of sorts, a promise to win her back. His seductive efforts to do just that had been disconcerting at first, but they had worked. Dear heaven, how well they had worked. He had used her body's yearning for the intoxication of his touches against her.

Her desire to believe in him had led her to self-delusion. She had ignored her instincts. All along they had told her that it was unlikely that Steven had spent the past eleven years or so pining away for her, no matter what he said. After all, it wasn't as though they'd been separated by a tragic fate or some great natural disaster. He'd chosen to leave. Even after he'd returned nearly three years ago, he had done nothing to make amends, nothing to draw her back into his life. There clearly had been no urgent sentiment on his part.

So why now? she wondered.

Burned once, she approached his motives cynically. Perhaps there was some new development scheme afoot, some plan that would require her property for success. He'd gotten hundreds of acres dirt cheap years ago by buying up family farms that were in financial trouble. A man capable of capitalizing on others' difficulties was ruthless enough to try anything. How far would he have been willing to go? Marriage? Perhaps his only intention had been to insinuate himself into her life until the time came when her own disaster struck. Fortunately for him, he hadn't had long to wait.

In her case, though, she vowed that this time he had met his match. Her father had held out eleven years ago, and despite the setback of the storm damage, she was in an even better position to hold out now.

Unbeknownst to Steven she had studied hard at agricultural extension classes. She had learned the lessons well, and the past few years had been good. Her cornfields had yielded the best crops ever. Even last year when she had spent a lot to improve the farm's technology and equipment and hire reliable workers to assist Logan, she had squeaked by in the black. Steven himself had told her that Mr. Hogan was proud of her accomplishments. The banker was unlikely to refuse her additional money to put things back on track in the spring. Maybe she could even get a late crop in and salvage something this year.

She'd promised herself that someday she would buy back the land she'd been forced to sell to Steven. It was the goal that had driven her ever since that humiliating day in the bank. She would not compound the serious, if unavoidable mistake she had made then by giving in to his charm now and selling him the rest. Instead, she would concentrate on discovering his real motives.

When the phone began ringing again, as it had all through the night, she ignored it. It continued incessantly, until finally she snatched it up and snapped, "Leave me alone!"

"Lara?" The gruff, distinctive voice of Terry Simmons sounded uncertain.

Lara sighed. "Terry, I'm sorry."

"Are you okay?"

"I've been better," she replied honestly.

"I heard the storm hit pretty hard out your way. How are things?"

"The house and barn are okay. The fields took the worst of it."

"Is there anything I can do?"

"No, thanks. I'm about to go into town to take care of some errands. I'll probably stop in at the bank to see how things stand there. I should be able to see from Mr. Hogan's reception how much trouble I'm really in."

"Why don't we meet for lunch? It sounds as though your spirits could use a little boosting."

Lara hesitated, then realized she needed Terry Simmons unquestioning comfort and perhaps even a little motherly advice. "Beaumont's at noon?"

"I'll see you there."

As soon as Lara had hung up, she left the house and drove straight to the county courthouse to check on recent land purchases and zoning requests.

At the courthouse she found Franklin Dennison with his bifocals sitting on the tip of his long, thin nose. He was surrounded by huge, dusty volumes of county land records. He blinked when she spoke to him, then smiled in recognition, deep lines furrowing his narrow face.

"Lara, what brings you over this way? We don't see much of you in town this time of year. You're usually too busy with the farm. The girls still visiting?"

"No. They went back to Kansas City with Tommy and Megan."

He shook his head disapprovingly. "Seems like a mighty long way to go. Families wander too much these days if you ask me."

"It's a good opportunity for Tommy, and to tell you the truth, I think he wanted to get out of my hair. Even though he wanted no part of living on the farm anymore, he had his own ideas about running the place. As long as he was here, we were bound to butt heads about it. Greg's not like that. I doubt if he'd notice if I let the whole place go to seed, unless it interfered with the work he does in that studio of his down in Columbus."

"Never did figure out where that boy got such an artistic streak," Franklin said. "Your daddy couldn't even plant corn in a straight line, much less draw one, and your mama was as sensible and down-to-earth as they come."

"But I found some of Mama's sketches after she died. Her doodles she called them. They were good. It's too bad she never really developed her talent."

"Her family was all that mattered to her. She'd be mighty proud of you, Lara. Those boys turned out to be fine men, thanks to you. You'll make a good mama one of these days."

"I did what I had to do," she said, suddenly becoming impatient with the idle gossip. Franklin apparently heard the slight snap in her voice.

"You didn't come in here for a pat on the head from me, did you, gal?" he said, taking no offense. "What can I help with?"

"I need to look at your records of land transactions."

He brushed a thick lock of grey hair back from his face and squinted at her. "Lordy, we got a lot of those. How far back you want to go?"

"Maybe the last five years."

"Anything in particular you're looking for?"

"Nothing exactly. Just a hunch I want to check out."

Two hours later she was exhausted, thirsty and practically cross-eyed from reading through the files. She'd found Steven's name on the deeds for a lot of property in the county, but it was scattered. Other than the housing development he'd put together eleven years ago, she couldn't find any logical pattern to suggest that he was planning another project of any kind. Nor had any zoning requests been filed to turn the residential and farmland properties he'd bought into shopping centers, industrial parks or even apartment complexes.

Sighing, she thanked Franklin and walked across the street to the newspaper office. Peter Grimes, the editor of the weekly, had gone to school with her. He'd gone on to Ohio State, majored in journalism, and then taken over the paper his father had founded. The family now owned similar local papers throughout the northwest section of the state.

She found Peter in the print shop in the back, moving galleys of type around on the forms for this week's edition.

"You look busy," she said when he finally looked up and saw her watching him.

He grimaced. "Matt has the flu. Now I ask you, who gets the flu in the summer? You're supposed to get it in February when it's dreary and you can recuperate in front of a fire with bowls of chicken soup. This time of year all you can do is lie around and get heat rash to go along with it.''

"I gather his absence means you have to paste up the pages yourself.''

"I do if I want the paper to come out tomorrow. Care to help?''

"I'd be happy to if I didn't think you'd wind up with the headline announcing the state fair over Tiffany Wyatt's obituary on page six.''

"Believe me, that's the least of my worries,'' he said wearily. "If you didn't come to help, what did you come for?''

"I was going to buy you a cup of coffee and pick your brain.''

His eyes brightened. "With a Danish? Don't you dare tease me, Lara Danvers. I've been here since dawn with nothing more than that black goo that my wife tries to pass for coffee.''

Lara laughed at his wistful tone. "Just to show you what a sport I can be, I'll go buy takeout and bring it back.''

Twenty minutes later amid blissful sighs of gratitude, Peter was eating his second cheese Danish as he continued to work on the pages. "Okay,'' he said when he'd swallowed the last bite and taken a long sip of the fragrant, rich coffee from Beaumont's, "my brain is yours.''

Lara plunged right in. "Is there much development going on in the county these days?''

"You've seen the shopping center out on the highway, and there are a couple of office buildings here in town. Nothing fancy. Why?"

"I'm not talking about things already going up. I mean behind-the-scenes stuff. Talk of big plans. Maybe some new housing developments. Have you heard anything?"

He studied her quizzically. "What have you heard?"

Lara laughed. "Don't try turning the tables on me, Peter Grimes. I'm picking *your* brain."

"Sorry," he said with a grin. "Force of habit. Now let me think a minute. There are always rumors every time anyone buys land, but I haven't heard anything specific. Nothing I'd be sure enough of to print anyway."

"But you have heard some gossip?"

"That's all it was, Lara, gossip."

"Who did it involve?"

Peter stopped what he was doing and met her gaze. He sighed. "So, that's what this is all about. You still haven't forgotten, have you?"

"Forgotten what?"

"Steven Drake and what he did to you years ago."

She regarded him in astonishment, edged with embarrassment. "What do you know about that?"

"Oh, for heaven's sake, Lara, this is a small town. Besides that, I was Tommy's best friend. I was around when Drake left. I saw the way you were before you left for college, mooning around the farm all sad eyed. When you came back when your mother died, you were no better. The pain was still there. I'd hoped it was a thing of the past by now, especially since I saw the two of you together out at the farm when Kelly was trapped in that well.''

''We have been getting along okay.''

''Then why all the questions?''

''I was just wondering,'' she said defensively.

''And I'm the editor of the *New York Times*,'' he retorted. ''You're not fooling me.''

He regarded her seriously. ''Let me give you a piece of advice, Lara. If you're thinking of trying to get even with him in some crazy way, forget it. He's a popular man around here now, a good man by all accounts. He's helped more than one person out and asked nothing in return. If you want to know something about Steven's plans, ask him. Don't catch your friends—his friends—in the middle.''

''Ask him,'' she muttered as she crossed the street to Beaumont's. Certainly it would be the direct approach, the one most likely to get answers. But would they be answers she could trust? Besides, the idea of confronting Steven was daunting. Just the thought of being in the same room with him made her heartbeat skip erratically, and once again, if honesty was to prevail, the reaction wasn't caused entirely by anger.

''Who put that stormy expression in your eyes?'' Terry inquired when she joined her in a booth by the window. ''Never mind. Let me guess. Steven?''

''Why would you say that? Isn't losing most of my crop justification for gloom?''

Terry nodded. ''Would be for some folks, but I'm guessing that's the sort of storm you can weather, if you'll pardon a terrible pun. Nope. This has to be a man-woman thing. What's he done?"

Lara considered whether or not to laugh off Terry's incredibly accurate guess, then decided against it. This certainly wasn't something she could call Tommy and Megan to discuss. They were all for her getting rid of the farm and going back to school. They'd just tell her she was being a damn fool for turning Steven down, no matter why he'd made the offer.

Finally she took a deep breath. "He wants me to go back to medical school."

Terry's brown eyes widened dramatically. "What an awful man!"

Lara stared at her, then caught the twitching of her lips. "Okay. You're making fun of me. I know that doesn't sound like much, but there's more. Since I refuse to accept money from him to do it, he offered to buy the farm."

"I think I'm beginning to see the problem. You don't want to sell, not even if it means getting the career you always wanted."

Lara shook her head. "I'm not so sure I even want that anymore," she said slowly, surprised herself by the admission. "I mean when the subject first came up, I toyed with it. Becoming a doctor was real important to me at one time, but I think the truth of the matter is that I really like farming. In spite of everything, I like the challenge of it."

"If you can say that after nearly getting wiped out yesterday, then I've got to believe it's true. So why don't you just tell Steven that?"

Unbidden, tears sprang to Lara's eyes. She swallowed hard, forcing the words past the lump in her throat. "Because I'm not so sure whether it's my happiness Steven wants or the farm."

"Oh," Terry whispered softly. "Oh my."

"Exactly."

Suddenly Lara felt a hand on her shoulder. She hadn't a doubt in the world as to its owner, especially with Terry looking more nervous than a kid caught with her hand in the cookie jar.

"Lara," Steven said. To her amazement there was anger underlying the smooth tone of his voice. She dared a glance up and caught the same coiled intensity in the set of his shoulders and in the flash of fire in his eyes. He nodded politely at Terry.

"Would you mind if I steal Lara away?" he said, already urging her from the booth. His touch was unyielding, though she did her best to resist.

"I'm not going anywhere with you," Lara snapped, just as Terry nodded agreeably.

"Oh, yes, you are." The words were spit out through clenched teeth. "Or we will have one hell of a scene right here."

Lara glowered at him mutinously, jerked free of his touch and marched from Beaumont's, her head held high. If Steven knew her as well as he thought he did, he'd have realized that the tilt of her head and the hard line of her jaw were a warning. Once on the street she whirled on him.

"Don't you ever, ever try that with me again," she seethed. "If you have something to say to me, call and make an appointment."

"I've been calling every hour on the hour since I left last night. Is your phone out of order?"

"No. There was no one I wished to speak to."

"Then you can't blame me for taking matters into my own hands, can you? Where would you like to finish this discussion?"

"I don't care to begin it."

"I wasn't asking your preference about that. We're going to talk. If you don't pick the location, I will."

"Here will be fine."

"I have too much to say to do it in the middle of the street." He clasped her hand and started walking. "It seems I'm always dragging you off to the town square to talk. Has it occurred to you how much more pleasant our lives would be, if you were more amenable?"

"I am amenable. You're the one who's an arrogant, hotheaded son—"

"Careful," he warned. "My temper is already at the breaking point."

"And mine is past it."

"So I noticed last night." He gestured to an empty bench. "Or would you prefer to go back to our favorite tree?"

"This will do." She kept a careful distance between them.

"Let's start with last night," he suggested. "Why did my offering to buy your farm send you into such a tizzy?"

Lara sat stubbornly silent.

"Don't make me lose my patience."

"I haven't seen any evidence that you have any."

"Lara!" His voice rose ominously.

"All right!" she shouted right back. "It's your motive that worries me."

There was genuine puzzlement in his eyes. "My motive?"

"Yes. Why did you make the offer?"

"So you'd have the money to go back to school," he responded immediately. There wasn't even a flicker of hesitation in his eyes. "Do you have a problem with that?"

"Oh, yes," she said with barely concealed fury. "For starters, I don't believe it."

He appeared honestly stunned by her attitude. "Why on earth not? It's the truth."

She hesitated for just an instant, confused by his reaction. Not even his voice had wavered. If he was acting, he was doing a good job.

"Don't insult my intelligence," she retorted. "You don't go around buying up land for some altruistic reason. You're a businessman. You make your decisions because they're good for you. You wanted my land so badly eleven years ago, you seduced an innocent kid to try to get it. Why should I believe for one moment that things are any different now? Your tactics certainly haven't changed."

His complexion paled, except for two spots of color high on his cheeks. He rose to his feet, towering over her. The cold look on his face made her quake inside.

"That's what you think of me?" His voice was low, but it cut through her like the lash of a whip. "You think I'm capable of using you to get what I want?"

Despite a sudden wave of uncertainty, she met his furious gaze boldly. "Yes."

"I see." He shook his head. Suddenly the anger was gone, replaced by sorrow. His voice fell to a ragged whisper. "You don't know me at all."

Eleven

Steven turned to walk away as Lara stared after him in stunned silence. His back was ramrod straight, his step brisk. He never once looked back.

His leaving had a quiet air of finality about it that shook her far more than his angry words. Beyond all else, it penetrated her righteous indignation and left her in doubt. Somehow she sensed that after this, his pride would never allow him to return to risk more such accusations. With a sense of amazement, she realized that she had hurt him deeply with her sharp tongue and blind outrage. Could she have wounded him so if he didn't care for her just a little?

And there was more. Was it at all possible that she had wronged him? He hadn't exactly denied her charges. He had disdained to acknowledge them at all.

All she knew, when sensation returned to replace shock, was that she ached inside. With her own anger fading, she was left with doubts and a terrifying, yearning emptiness that she knew from experience only Steven could fill.

Finally she became aware of her surroundings. The park was busy at this time of day—mothers pushing carriages, children on bikes, employees on their lunch breaks, all creating a cheerful, noisy atmosphere that counterpointed her somber mood.

Slowly other things registered. The ground was still slightly damp from yesterday's rain. The air was heavy with humidity and rich with the scent of the rose bushes that spilled petals over the ground. In this wreckage of the storm there was at least a delicate, colorful patchwork. Sunlight played tag with huge fluffy white clouds. It was a lovely summer day, but it meant little to her without Steven by her side to share it.

Was this the way she was doomed to spend her life? Would she always be alone in a colorless world because the man who had brought brightness into her life had gone? No, she thought, coming to a decision. She'd sacrificed enough. If there were answers to be had to her questions, she would have them. And if she owed him an apology for doubting him, she would make it.

And what, a voice nagged, what if she had been right? She thought about that and dismissed it for the moment. She would deal with that possibility when—and if—she was forced to. In the meantime, sitting in this park was the last thing she ought to be doing. There were no answers for her here.

She leaped to her feet and went back to her car. Exhilarated by a heady mix of anger and determination, she managed to keep her foot light on the accelerator until she reached the outskirts of town. Then she drove with reckless speed over the country roads leading back to Steven's property. She had the distinct feeling that she was traveling toward her destiny.

It had been the worst day of Steven's life. The pain that had cut through him at Lara's accusations went deeper and hurt far more than even the terrible years of separation. That she could think that he would seduce her only to get her land made him question her love as nothing else ever had.

And still he wanted her. His body's responses had not caught up with his mind, which told him again and again to let it end with some measure of dignity on his part. He had verbally brawled and fought his way to the top in business. He had no intention of doing the same in romance. If she trusted him so little, what sort of relationship could they possibly have?

And yet he couldn't forget that first glimpse of her in Beaumont's this afternoon. She had looked sad and lost and lonely. She had also appeared infinitely desirable. It had sent a surge of heated blood racing through him. Even as he had walked away from her in the park to satisfy his pride, his body and soul had cried out with another need.

In all the years of remembering Lara, nothing had prepared him for the shock of her cruel cynicism. She

had always represented gentleness and understanding
and, above all, the kind of unquestioning, generous,
passionate love he'd never before experienced. However, her actions today had nothing to do with love.
They spoke only of distrust and disillusion.

*Maybe if she'd allowed herself to grieve... Maybe
then she wouldn't have become so bitter and withdrawn.*

Megan's words came back to him suddenly. Was
Lara's behavior today part of that pattern established
years ago? Certainly that's when he'd sown the seeds
of distrust. Until now, though, he'd had no idea that
they'd taken hold so well. He'd thought he'd overcome all of her doubts and suspicions, but when put
to the test, eleven years of pain had overcome a com-
paratively short time of loving.

When he finally arrived at home, he prowled
through the house, unable to stay still, uncomfortable with his whirling thoughts.

"Have you had lunch?" Mrs. Marston asked,
catching him on what must have been his dozenth trip
from living room to terrace and back again.

"I'm not hungry," he growled, stalking back outside. She followed him with dogged determination.

"Some iced tea, then? It's very humid this afternoon."

He paused and glowered fiercely. "I don't want any
tea, either."

"What about—"

"Dammit, I just want to be left alone."

Her eyebrows had risen at that, but she'd gone back
to the kitchen without lecturing on either his lan-

guage or his surly attitude. He wondered how long such docility would last. She'd probably leave all the seasoning out of his dinner tonight just to make a point.

Steven carried his briefcase out to the patio and took out the papers he'd had prepared earlier in the week after his conversation with Megan. He'd meant them to be something positive for Lara. There was so much he wanted to do to make life easier for her. This was supposed to be a start. Instead, the papers had become the symbol of a relationship between two people who apparently didn't understand each other at all.

Lara brought the car to a squealing halt in front of Steven's house, sending gravel flying. She got out and slammed the door.

She raced up the steps and repeatedly punched the doorbell, listening to it echo through the house. When Mrs. Marston opened the door, Lara managed a brief smile, then demanded, "Where is he?"

"On the terrace." As Lara started through the house, Mrs. Marston called out to her. "Be careful, Ms. Danvers. He's in a foul mood."

Adopting an air of bravado, Lara grinned at her and waved the mood off as being of no consequence. "I know," she said with glib confidence, ignoring the queasiness in her stomach.

However, when she reached the French doors that opened onto the terrace, she hesitated. Steven was sitting in the sun, his head bowed, rubbing his temples. His briefcase was open. Papers were lying untouched on the terrace. He looked utterly defeated and incredibly vulnerable.

"Steven."

His shoulders tensed. He lifted his head at the whisper of his name and stared at her. An eloquent look of longing filled his eyes, only to be quickly replaced by a veil of disinterest. He waited, not saying a word.

"Can we finish that talk?" she asked quietly.

He shrugged in an elaborate show of indifference. "I thought you were finished."

"So did I," she said. "It's possible, though, that I jumped to a hasty conclusion."

"It is possible," he concurred, a wry twist to his lips.

"I want to go back to what happened eleven years ago. You've told me why you left, and I believe you."

"Thank you."

There was an unmistakable edge of sarcasm in his voice that almost made her falter in her resolve. She lifted her chin and met his gaze evenly. "Why did you seduce me in the first place?"

That brought a spark of amusement to his eyes. "As I recall, it was you who did the seducing."

Her face burned at the accuracy of his memory. "I don't mean just that night at the stream. I mean everything, all the attention, the gifts. It was all part of the seduction."

"Would you believe me if I told you it was because I couldn't help myself?"

Her eyebrows arched doubtfully. Though his words had the ring of truth about them, she couldn't imagine Steven Drake ever not being in control of his feelings or his actions. Especially back then, when there had been an undeniably hard edge about him. It had been easy to believe that that man had the ruthlessness to use her, but this one? Could the man who watched her now with so much emotion on his face have done that? She waited impatiently for his explanation, praying for one that would exonerate him.

"From the moment I saw you," he began softly, "I was just a little bit enchanted. It was like having a magical spell cast around me. There was a mysteriously compelling air of innocence and boldness about you that drew me from the first. I had to know you."

His eyes never left hers as he spoke. Breathless, she whispered, "What about the land?"

"It had nothing to do with that. When I first saw you, I didn't have the vaguest idea of your name or where you lived or anything else about you. I only saw a lovely young woman I wanted to know."

"But there came a time when you did know who I was," she persisted.

Steven sighed. "Lara, I am not going to deny that I came to this part of the state looking for land. I felt there was a potential for growth here, that families from Toledo would be looking for a more peaceful environment as that city grew. Speculating in land is what my company does, in addition to putting together development deals and doing engineering studies."

"So you stole from the farmers to make yourself rich." She was unable to restrain the bitterness she'd felt for so long.

"I stole nothing," he retorted. "You were eighteen years old, Lara. You hated the farm back then. You had no interest in farming or in the people who did it. Yet you reacted emotionally to what was—for them and for me—a satisfactory business arrangement."

She flinched as the accuracy of his charge hit home. He wasn't finished yet, either.

"How many of those families did you ever talk to?" he asked. "How many did you ask if they could have survived another year without financial collapse? Did you ever once stop to consider that some of them had been beaten by the land just as your own father and mother had been? Some of their sons and daughters were just as desperate as you were to move on."

"Are you trying to tell me that your motives were purely altruistic?"

"Of course not. But the deals were fair. They got money and an opportunity to build new lives, even job training if they wanted it. There's not a farmer among them who would say otherwise."

It was true, she realized suddenly. She had never heard the farmers speak negatively about Steven. If anything, they had welcomed him into the community far more warmly than she had. She had seen for herself the depth of their respect for him when they all worked side by side to save Kelly.

"You tried to get my father's land, too."

"He and I discussed it on several occasions, yes. This land is in an ideal location for one of those suburban communities I wanted to create. He didn't want to sell. He felt very strongly that it was the only legacy he had to leave to you and your brothers."

Tears sprang to Lara's eyes as his words recalled her mother's deathbed wish that she save her father's legacy. "He loved this land," she said with quiet simplicity. "Despite all it took from him, he loved it."

"Yes, he did."

"But you still tried to force him to sell."

Steven reached out to her and took her hand, pulling her closer. She went reluctantly, disturbed that his touch could stir her so easily. A warm glow was already beginning to build inside, outshining the doubts.

"No, Lara," he said. "I told him my offer would always be good, but I never tried to force him to sell, not after he told me why he wanted to keep the land."

She searched his expression for any sign of a lie and found only compassion and gentleness and honesty. "Why did you insist on buying part of it three years ago?"

"Because I'd heard the kind of financial trouble you were in, and I knew you'd never accept a loan from me. It was the only way I could think of to protect the land for you."

"You did that, even knowing how it would look to me, that it would infuriate me?"

"I had to risk it. It seemed to be all you had that meant anything to you."

"And now?"

"I only offered to buy it, so that you could go back to school. Besides, with my own home right here next to it, it would go against my own best interests to develop it. In fact, my intention was to keep it and . . ." His voice trailed off uncertainly.

"And what?"

He lifted her hand to his lips and brushed a kiss across the knuckles, all the while keeping his eyes steadily on hers. The pace of her heart picked up as she waited.

"I was going to give it back to you—all of it—as a wedding present."

A mist of tears clouded Lara's vision, and her hands trembled.

"Lara?"

"I'm not sure I understand."

His lips curved into a provocative grin. "Oh, I think you probably do."

Her breathing became quick and shallow. Heat rushed to her cheeks. "Tell me."

"I was hoping that someday, after you became Dr. Lara Danvers, you'd also consent to becoming Mrs. Steven Drake."

"And what if I stay plain old farmer Lara Danvers?"

"You, my love, will never be plain," he said, drawing her onto his lap. Her arms instinctively circled his neck, and she took a leisurely survey of his face as he added, "As for your occupation, I don't care if you take up beekeeping. I still want you to be my wife."

Lara's pulse raced out of control then, and fire danced through her veins. Still, there was one thing Steven had never said. Not eleven years earlier. Not today. He had never said he loved her.

He had shown her, though. In so many ways he had shown her love time and again. Not just with his body, but in his tenderness, his supportiveness. He had been with her throughout the ordeal with Kelly. He had tried valiantly to lift her beyond depression when her nieces had left. He'd been by her side, helping and caring, in the horrible aftermath of the tornado. There had been real fear in his eyes when he had thought she might be seriously injured. Even now with the land, his gesture had been well-intentioned, loving. If the words of love didn't come as easily as the actions, she would have a lifetime to draw them from him.

He reached around her then and picked up a folder from the stack on the ground beside him. "Just in case you're having any lingering doubts," he said.

Lara opened the folder to the first page and found a contract calling for his purchase of the remainder of the Danvers' land. In a final clause it was noted that this land and his earlier purchase were to be held in trust for her and her heirs until such time as she and she alone should decide to sell it.

"When did you have this drawn up?"

"I called my lawyer after I left you last night. I'd guessed at least some of what was bothering you. This was the only way I could think of to convince you that my intentions were totally honorable. Now what about it? Do we have a deal?"

Heart soaring, Lara's lips curved into an impish smile. "Which deal is that? For the land?"

"To hell with the land," he growled. "You can have it, the money, anything I have. Are you going to marry me or not?"

"I would be proud to marry you, Steven Drake. Very proud."

"How soon?"

"Long engagements are nice."

"For whom?" he grumbled, his impatience bringing a soft smile to her lips.

"But then, we have had a rather extended courtship," she added thoughtfully.

"Does that mean we get time off for good behavior?"

"Something like that."

"How soon?" he repeated impatiently.

"Christmas?"

"That's months from now."

"I want to wait for Tommy and Megan and the girls to come back." She brushed a kiss across his lips, then dropped another one on his forehead. "I promise to make the wait worth your while."

His muscles tensed, and his arms tightened around her. She could feel the hurried beat of his heart beneath her fingers as he said, "In that case, I accept."

With that, he swept her into his arms and carried her up to his room. Their room. It was hours before Lara was aware of anything except the fire that raged in her body, the sweet throbbing that rose to an impatient demand before sending her off into aching ecstasy.

Life suddenly held the promise of spring all over again, the same eager anticipation and hope that marked all new beginnings. She knew now that the bonds between them were not flimsy. They were meant to hold for eternity.

As she sighed and curled herself into his waiting warmth, his breath whispered across her cheek, the words soft, but spoken without hesitation.

"I'll love you, Lara. For always."
For always.

*   *   *   *   *

READERS' COMMENTS ON SILHOUETTE DESIRES

"Thank you for Silhouette Desires. They are the best thing that has happened to the bookshelves in a long time."
—V.W.*, Knoxville, TN

"Silhouette Desires—wonderful, fantastic—the best romance around."
—H.T.*, Margate, N.J.

"As a writer as well as a reader of romantic fiction, I found DESIREs most refreshingly realistic—and definitely as magical as the love captured on their pages."
—C.M.*, Silver Lake, N.Y.

"I just wanted to let you know how very much I enjoy your Silhouette Desire books. I read other romances, and I must say your books rate up at the top of the list."
—C.N.*, Anaheim, CA

"Desires are number one. I especially enjoy the endings because they just don't leave you with a kiss or embrace; they finish the story. Thank you for giving me such reading pleasure."
—M.S.*, Sandford, FL

*names available on request

Keepsake

◆ Harlequin Books

You're never too young to enjoy romance. Harlequin for you . . . and Keepsake, young-adult romances destined to win hearts, for your daughter.

Pick one up today and start your daughter on her journey into the wonderful world of romance.

Two new titles to choose from each month.

FOUR UNIQUE SERIES
FOR EVERY WOMAN YOU ARE...

Silhouette Romance

Love, at its most tender, provocative,
emotional...in stories that will make you laugh and
cry while bringing you the magic of falling in love.

Silhouette Special Edition

Sophisticated, substantial and packed with
emotion, these powerful novels of life and love will
capture your imagination and steal your heart.

Silhouette Desire

Open the door to romance and passion. Humorous,
emotional, compelling—yet always a believable
and sensuous story—Silhouette Desire never
fails to deliver on the promise of love.

Silhouette Intimate Moments

Enter a world of excitement, of romance
heightened by suspense, adventure and the
passions every woman dreams of. Let us
sweep you away.

SILG-1R

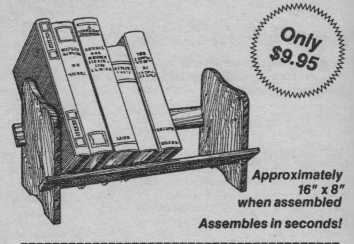

1989
IS THE YEAR
OF THE MAN!

What makes a romance? A special man, of course, and Silhouette Desire celebrates that fact with *twelve* of them! From Mr. January to Mr. December, every month spotlights the Silhouette Desire hero—our **MAN OF THE MONTH**.

Sexy, macho, charming, irritating...irresistible! Nothing can stop these men from sweeping you away. Created by some of your favorite authors, each man is custom-made for pleasure—*reading* pleasure—so don't miss a single one.

Diana Palmer kicks off the new year, and you can look forward to magnificent men from **Joan Hohl**, **Jennifer Greene** and many, many more. So get out there and find your man!

Silhouette Desire's

MAN OF THE MONTH...